THE DEATH OF OSCAR UZGALIS

THE DEATH OF OSCAR UZGALIS

The Olympic Gods on the Nature of Death

JOHN L. BOWMAN

CONTENTS

PROLOGUE

IT WAS OSCAR'S BEST FRIEND BENAS SAVICKIS'S DAY TO DIE. OSCAR and Benas had grown up together in Lithuania, had played together as children, had gone to school together, had hiked the hills around Palanga together, had experienced their first sex with girls on a double date, had been each other's best man at their weddings, and were godfathers to each other's children. Benas was twenty-five years old, a little overweight, easygoing, and well liked, with many friends.

They were playing their usual competitive game of basketball early Saturday morning when Oscar, while running up court and expecting Benas to pass him the ball, saw an unusual look of fear in his friend's face—a look he had never seen before. Oscar watched as Benas became unsteady, wobbled, and suddenly grabbed his chest. Then he screamed in pain as he collapsed on the floor. Hoping to help, Oscar ran to Benas as he writhed in pain, but all he could do was hold Benas's trembling and sweaty body and look into his terror-stricken face as his eyes rolled during his violent and spasmodic struggle with death. Oscar watched in fright as Benas's face suddenly turned ashen, his eyes glassed over, he gave a long, deep death-throe sigh, and his body went from stiff to limp as his muscles relaxed. Oscar slowly laid his dead friend's body down and could only stare in angst at the lifeless face that now no longer looked back at him.

A stranger frantically began pushing on Benas's chest until the medics arrived a few minutes later. Oscar watched as they jabbed a needle in his heart and filled it with some medicine then put paddles on his chest and gave him repeated shocks that made his body jump. After about five minutes of repeated efforts, the medics declared Benas dead and put his body in a plastic corpse sack.

Oscar was horrified. He had never seen a person die from a heart attack. Not only had he lost his best friend, he had also watched him die in excruciating pain. Oscar thought about how just a few minutes earlier Benas had been alive, talking and playing basketball, and now he was dead and gone forever. It was this awful experience that gave Oscar his deep fear of death.

CHAPTER 1

The Gods

THE MYTHOLOGICAL GODS OF ANCIENT GREECE WERE LYING ON their favorite lounge chairs high on Mt. Olympus discussing humans. This night they were having an unusually animated conversation about death and humans' fear of it. Kratos, the god of strength and power, asked why humans fear death so much. Meddling and opinionated Ares, god of chaos and war, said they fear death because they are impotent—they don't know what death is, and they have no control over whether they die. Zeus, the leader of the Olympic gods and god of lightning, thunder, and the heavens, said be quiet, Thanatos wanted to say something.

Thanatos, God of Death

Then Thanatos, the god of death, who had a Moses-like serious arrogant personality, son of Nyx the goddess of night and brother to Hypnos the god of sleep, said that Oscar Uzgalis had died last night. Thanatos said he had decided Oscar had suffered enough and it was time to put him out of his misery. He said humans are the longest-living mammals with a natural life span of 100 to 110 years.

Asclepius, the god of health and medicine, interrupted and said that assumes they take care of themselves and are lucky enough to avoid the many fatal sources of death. Hygeia, the goddess of cleanliness and hygiene, explained that Oscar had died young because he did not take care of himself physically or mentally. She said there are many ways humans die. Some contract slow, creeping diseases, some go mad, and in Benas's case, others put a vice grip on the heart, which is what also killed Oscar. Indeed, Thanatos added, he was lucky to live as long as he did, considering his many heart attacks.

Phobos, the God of Fear

Phobos, the god of fear and panic, responded to Thanatos and discussed humans' fear of death, and asked Thanatos if Oscar had overcome it. Oscar was like most humans because his greatest fear was death, unlike the other animals. This is why most humans live repressed, naked, fearful, and trembling lives alone, doomed to live in an overwhelmingly tragic and demonic world. Indeed, Phobos mused, it was Cicero who wisely wrote, *The best thing for humans is not to be born at all and the next best is to die as soon as possible.*

Unfortunately for Oscar, Thanatos responded, it took a long time for him to get over the fear of death. Indeed, he was first confronted with the reality of death during his first heart attack. Like most humans he had many strategies to help him forget about death, but its specter was too powerful for him to ignore, so over time he gradually accepted the notion that someday he would be nothing.

Athena, Goddess of Wisdom

Then Athena, the goddess of wisdom, said that is a shame, because it is only when humans accept death that they begin to live meaningful lives. The truth is they must reconcile themselves with becoming nothing before they can learn to live. Those who never learn this live strange and empty lives, as Oscar did most of his life. Their perpetual ignorant curiosity causes them to forever metaphysically wonder why they were born, who they are, why they are here, and what they are supposed to do. They live in a grey area, thinking there should be some meaning to it all but unable to discern it. They waste hours vainly endeavoring to qualify for immortality. And it is those who pursue the myth of being special with the most energy who burn with the brightest flame—only to become a cinder sooner. The irony is, the harder humans try to escape their condition to achieve meaning, the less meaning they get. What is the point? Why bother? Ultimately they all die and are forgotten when the race is over. There is simply no way to transcend the human condition and triumph over nature. There is no way out, and trying to be something special is a myth.

Most of Oscar's life was an example of why the inability to accept death causes meaningless lives. Much happens to your outlook on life when you have seen and accepted the abyss. What is truly meaningful, what values endure, and what the nature of happiness is become conspicuous. You become more intellectually critical of what parents, society, and school have told you to think. Unfortunately Oscar learned not to fear death late in life, which caused him to live a largely dull and meaningless one.

Oscar's Friends and Family Discuss Him

One of Oscar's character flaws was to think he was important—just listen to what his friends and family said about him after he died. Indeed, Plutus, the god of wealth, said some of Oscar's old Lithuanian friends, like Elijah Ballus, complained about having to go to his funeral. And Benas Prudius, who was a fellow employee at the civil service with Oscar approving visas, was excited to think he might get Oscar's job and the higher salary that goes along with it. Connor and Cara Kelly, Irish friends Oscar had acquired through his Irish wife Madeline, complained about having to send a condolence letter to Oscar's family. Many human problems arise from money, to which Nemesis, goddess of retribution and vengeance, said yes, take Oscar's former close friend Adomas Urbonas, for example. They had a falling out and long acrimonious feud over money Adomas claimed Oscar owed him. Now he is giddy with joy at Oscar's death. He told everyone he was glad Oscar was dead and gone.

The god Priapus, god of gardens and fertility (best known for having an enormous penis), spoke up and said Oscar's family was mostly callous about his death. Ares, who thought Priapus was an arrogant bully, said Priapus, I have seen your penis, and it is just not that impressive. Irritated, Priapus ignored him and said Oscar's brother Domantas Uzgalis had said Oscar was not much of a brother because he was consumed with himself. Domantas's wife Lina was only interested in any inheritance Oscar may have left them.

Oscar had three children with Madeline, a girl and two boys. All of them had died before Oscar, so theirs are the thoughts they had about their father and husband when he was alive and they thought they would outlive him. Put another way, they assumed Oscar would die before they did. Megan Uzgalis, his only daughter, had nothing but scorn for her father. She said she knew she had been rebellious and that had caused her father's disapproval, but she did not care. She thought he was mean and bossy and did not like her much. She said she would be glad when he was gone. Priapus noted that children are a mixed blessing. Sometimes parents and children like each other and sometimes not. Oscar had two boys, Mehal and Maurice. Mehal said he would be rather indifferent to his father's death because his father had always been indifferent to him. Maurice was the lone exception. He was an intelligent, philosophic lad who could see the big picture and understand his father's weakness. He said he loved his father and thought he would miss him in spite of his flaws.

Oscar's wife Madeline Uzgalis had mixed feelings about his death. On one hand she said she would be grieved over losing her lifelong partner, husband, and the father of her children, who she had gone through so much with. On the other hand, she thought she would be elated by the prospect of freedom, fewer duties, and the disappearance of the dreaded role of wife. Madeline thought she would be relieved at Oscar's death. It seemed none of Oscar's friends and family would be sad to see him go.

Hades, God of the Dead and Underworld

It was then that Hades, the powerful god of the dead and the Underworld, and brother to Zeus and Poseidon, said, unbeknownst to Thanatos, Oscar is not dead. Just before he went out of existence, I resuscitated him. With the help of the Grim Reaper, put him in Limbo, that border place between Heaven and Hell. He is now waiting for your decision whether to send him to Purgatory for eternal punishment for his vices or to Heaven for his virtues, where he would live in eternal joy with the Gods. In the meantime, you can talk with him.

CHAPTER 2
Fear of Death

Irritated that Hades had tricked him, Thanatos ruminated on death and said it is such a powerful, awesome, black, cold, brooding, sinister, and threatening real thing. There is nothing like it in all human experience. It is so opaque, esoteric, and secret humans cannot comprehend it. Their minds can only imagine eternity, infinity, and death; they can only wonder and suffer under such incomprehensible and foreboding thoughts. All humans live with this unavoidable subterranean knowledge that they will someday be nothing, which constantly reminds them that their lives are pointless and nothing ultimately matters.

The famous human philosopher Immanuel Kant thought a sublime mystery of creation was human consciousness—the state of being awake and aware of one's surroundings, perception of something, or just awareness. Humans wonder how this happens. Is it something metaphysical, like an observing soul, or is it just the physical brain perceiving through the senses? Whichever the case, it is this consciousness that causes humans to experience a unique terror that leads to a profound dilemma.

All animals except humans, from insects to crocodiles or fish to elephants, are unaware that they will die, which brings a certain kind of unreflective contentedness. Certainly, they all have the instinct to survive, but this is not the same as the awareness of becoming nothing. They remain blithely unaware of their death. Humans have no such luxury, because their consciousness makes them aware that they will die, a thought that haunts and torments them. This is humans' terrible burden—to know they will die.

Knowing they will die makes humans strange beings indeed—a creature that is noble and base, unique and common, Godlike and brutelike. On one hand they are highly evolved, reasoning creatures capable of transcending the secret laws of nature, but on the other they are creatures just like all other animals, that defecate, die, and rot in the ground. So their dilemma is that they are out of nature due to their mind but hopelessly within nature due to their body, a kind of splendidly unique being that rots. Humans live in the stars and contemplate universals but depend on a breathing, sweating body that disappears forever. To make matters worse, they know there is no way to escape their predicament, which makes them feel helpless. This is the price humans pay for being highly evolved: they attain more in life than the other animals, which only burdens them with the knowledge of their own death.

Phobos on Humans' Fear of Death

Phobos told Thanatos that his explanations for how death affects humans failed to mention the single most profound consequence: it is consciousness that makes them aware of their death, which brings the fear of death that causes humans the most anxiety. It pervades their lives and causes them a deep existential panic. Their eminent psychologist Sigmund Freud was wrong in thinking it was the repression of sexuality that caused their greatest angst, but he was on the right track when he described the elaborate defenses humans imagine, like religion, to avoid it. Throughout human history the one thing that has animated people, the great constants and things few talk about, are decay and death. It has always been humans' greatest fear and anxiety.

Phobos on Why Humans Fear Death

There are many reasons why humans, like Oscar Uzgalis, fear death. One is the fear of pain from illness that often accompanies dying, Phobos continued. This is certainly a real fear due to a physical cause—this is a fear not created by the mind or imagination. The lung cancer patient enduring suffocation, the dying pedestrian hit by a car feeling multiple stings and pangs, and the heart attack victim with the excruciating feeling of an elephant on their chest are real physical sources of unhappiness. Not much can be said to ameliorate this fear other than not all deaths involve pain, such as a dying person in a coma, and thanks to modern medicine, there exists today a variety of analgesics that lessen or eliminate pain. Indeed, it should be pointed out that death itself does not cause pain; it is illness that causes pain. Death just hangs around and in a way is the ultimate analgesic because it is a release from pain. I should also mention that many societies today allow those who have terminal illnesses the legal option to commit suicide—hence death can be used to avoid the pain of an illness.

Another reason is the finality of death; nothing in human lives compares to such permanence. Humans are used to dynamic, changing lives where they progress through school, leave their home and parents, meet a future spouse, and start a family, and sometimes they experience natural disasters like earthquakes, forest fires, or pandemics, all while they are slowly aging. Death changes all this because there are no changes in eternity, which is an unsettling thought. Humans are also used to living in the future and making plans for it, but with death there is no more future and no need for plans.

Many fear death because it is inevitable. It is going to happen whether they like it or not. Humans are used to some degree of control over their lives, like what to eat, whether to marry, and when to get out of bed, but with death there are no choices. They are faced with the truism that not everything is possible and there is nothing they can do about it. As living creatures, there is no way they can avoid death, and there is no way to overcome their existence. They cannot excuse themselves from life to avoid death. Indeed, as the Stoic philosopher Epictetus once wrote: *Death and disease will overtake you, whatever you are doing.*

Perhaps above all, humans fear the unknown. They fear that which they cannot know or comprehend, and death is one of their greatest incomprehensible unknowns. No one who has died has ever returned to verifiably explain what happened to them. Certainly, people live with many unknowns, such as what the future holds, but death is the ultimate end—there is nothing beyond it. So humans conjure heavens and afterlives in order to ameliorate their fear, but this is just their overactive imagination. Philosopher Søren Kierkegaard in *Three Discourses on Imagined Occasions* wrote that death is not a monster except for the imagination. Things people cannot understand incite fear, which their imagination magnifies beyond proportion—and death magnifies it the most.

Humans invest a lot in their bodies during their lifetimes. They feed them, keep them warm, exercise them, medicate them, eliminate from them, and sexually satisfy them, but when they die, it just becomes meat for worms, which disturbs them. They are forced to imagine their warm bodies going into the cold, cold ground to decay, rot, and be consumed by microbes. They become disillusioned with their once-cared-for bodies and experience a kind of terror at become carrion—corpses.

Further, knowing that when they die they will become nothing causes great fear, angst, and unhappiness in humans. To become nothing is a fearsome thought to them. None of them can conceive of their own nonexistence. It is like trying to describe what being unconscious or explaining a unicorn: they cannot. Humans simply cannot conceive what is like to be annihilated. Just recall Marcus Aurelius's comment near the end of his life long ago: *You will die, and shortly after, not even your name will be left.*

Some fear the end of their experience of living. They are accustomed to life and naturally want to preserve it. People feel remorseful about losing experience in two ways: the loss of experience for themselves and the loss of experience of others. When people think about losing their experience, it is usually fear of the loss of their experience. They are, in effect, saying goodbye to themselves and mourning the loss of the self. This often translates into the desire to experience sensation in death in order to make them survive. But this is a waste of time, because it is impossible to experience being dead or to survive it.

Losing the experience of others, on the other hand, is the fear of losing loved ones and friends. People lament leaving other people. They are sad at having to say goodbye to their parents, spouses, children, and old friends. They also mourn not knowing what will happen to them. One mother who had spent a lifetime caring for children lamented death because she would no longer learn their future lives and fates.

Phobos said these are the reasons humans fear death, which only incites their imaginations to create elaborate myths like afterlives, heaven, and reincarnation to ameliorate their fear. The consequence of this is that humans live in denial attempting to deny their grotesque fate, but these metaphysical myths only detach them from reality and suspend them in an illusionary world where they pretend not to be mad. I will discuss these myths, or strategies, that pervade all human individuals and societies later.

Athena on the Price Humans Pay for Their Burden

Athena said Phobos certainly knows human fears, mainly because he made them. Indeed, she continued, I find it ironic that Phobos, who instills fear in others, is himself anxiety riven, jumpy, and easily spooked. In spite of his weaknesses, he is right, but he fails to explain how humans pay a much higher price for their consciousness, knowledge, and subsequent fear of death. It is the source of their persistent repression that causes universal anxiety, denial, and a strange madness. They ignore the devastating and terrifying reality of death, which makes routine, automatic, secure, and self-confident activity impossible. It is a kind of madness, and its symptoms are aptly described by what many of their psychologists call the anal stage. Humans see repulsive, disgusting excrement come from their anus, which they associate with decay and death. They all know they defecate and die, but they rarely talk about it and pretend it does not happen; thus, they live a lie in perpetual denial.

So repressed madness is the way it is for most humans, but it does not have to be that way. A profound peace is possible if humans could learn to renounce the world and themselves, surrender the meaning of life to the powers of creation, and humbly accept the fact that they die. When they learn that the point of being here is to live their lives, use themselves up, and then die, they learn the way to avoid the terror of death. Recall Seneca's words; *Round it off with a good ending.* Accept death and round your life off with a good one.

CHAPTER 3
Oscar Uzgalis

T HANATOS SAID TO THE OTHER GODS THAT WE ALL HAVE OUR opinions about humans and their fear of death, but let's ask recently deceased Oscar Uzgalis what he thinks.

Oscar's Monologue

Oscar was indignant when the Grim Reaper brought him in. Why on earth do you gods want to talk with me, Oscar Uzgalis? I have led a rather dull, uninteresting, and commonplace life as a petty bureaucrat with no power. You gods, on the other hand, have really exciting lives. Apollo, the god of the sun and atmosphere, creates storms that sink hundreds of ships and drown thousands of sailors. Ares, the meddling god of chaos and war, foments conflicts between human societies, destroying villages and killing hundreds of thousands of civilians and soldiers. To make things even more belittling, you gods are keeping me in this very strange place, Limbo, while debating whether to send me to Heaven or Hell. Why do you bother?

Oscar on His Heritage

I come from a long line of Lithuanian Uzgalis. Many of my ancestors were aristocrats, clergy, scholars, and a few rich burgers, but the family's fortunes declined. I was born in the town of Palanga on the Baltic Sea to Jonas and Regina Uzgalis. My father worked as a collier, and my mother took in laundry and tailoring to help make ends meet. I loved my parents—my father was kind and gentle, and my mother's name meant "saint," which she was. They died long ago, and I miss them terribly. I grew up in a lower-class neighborhood, played with my best friend Benas Savickis, hiked the hills around Palanga in the fall and spring, and swam in the Baltic Sea in the summer. I decided I had enough of schooling when I graduated from high school at eighteen and took an extended trip through Europe for fun. It was in Dublin that I met and fell in love with Madeline Walsh, a dark-haired Irish beauty with a strong character and stronger opinions. We married and moved to Galway, Ireland, where we started a family.

I should mention that my family's name Uzgalis means "beyond the end," which brought a natural and historic dilemma to my family's and my existence. Many of my ancestors were Catholic clergy believing in an afterlife and Heaven, or beyond the end, and some others were philosophy professors, like William Uzgalis, who were more materialistic and naturalistic, with no belief in the beyond. The tension caused by this dichotomy of views brought discord, mental illness, and a few suicides to my lineage. It brought me nothing but confusion. I have to admit that my intelligence is average, so I spent a good part of my life struggling to decide if there was a Heaven. I will tell you what I decided later.

Oscar on His Life and Character

I am the first to admit I could have led a better life. (The goddess Athena muttered, That is an understatement.) I now know thoughtful people grapple with many profound issues in life, like death, family, society, forgiveness, and what constitutes a meaningful life. If I had just taken the time to ponder, I would have also considered these things, but instead I wasted most of my life being worried about trivial things like money, career, aging, and especially the fear of dying. Being in Limbo, I now see how petty my life has been.

I lived a shallow life as a shallow thinker. I never discerned important life goals to achieve, like education, so I had low aspirations with low goals. How I looked, who I knew, where I lived, how to get money, and seeking the next sensual pleasure preoccupied me. I was a coward living an ordinary life with empty, artificial, vague, and meaningless aspirations.

At this point Dionysus, also known as Bacchus, the god of wine and pleasure, said to the other gods, I can assure you that in his youth Oscar lived a dissipated life, visiting brothels and staying out late drinking wine like a hedonist in pursuit of pleasure.

I also spent most of my life being totally self-absorbed and not other-regarding, continued Oscar. I thought I was important and the center of the universe. I had little time for people who did not advance my interests, and my eyes would glaze over when anyone talked for more than thirty seconds. I never really listened to people because I was always thinking about what I wanted to say next. I was obsessed and preoccupied with myself and my own petty desires and problems.

Oscar on Society

Early in life I bought into thoughtless, common, and mundane bourgeois class morality and standards of success. I unthinkingly allowed established empty and vacuous norms to run my life. I worked at a menial job I hated, I bought a house and took on a mortgage I did not want, I coveted my neighbor's wife because I wanted more sensual pleasure, I became a social climber endeavoring to have the right friends, I angled to get into the right clubs, and I strove to give the best parties. I spent a lot of time showing off for people at the top, who just looked down on me, or bragging to people at the bottom, who only envied and despised me. I was driven to make more money and have a better house and car than my neighbors. I valued money more than my friends. Domas Meka was one of my oldest friends until we had an argument over some money I owed him, which resulted in a lifelong estrangement and feud.

Plutus, the god of wealth, said, Yes, and you looked like a damn fool. Few liked you and nobody revered you.

Eventually I learned that allowing societal goals to compel me to do what I don't want to is like a living death, and letting society determine my success comes at a great moral cost. It's a hollow, insincere life full of silent resentment and anger, which is almost worse than death. I will describe some meaningful ways to think and live I discovered late in life later.

Oscar on His Family

I was not a successful family man. I fell in love with Madeline and wanted to be with her, but I did not want to marry because I did not want the obligations families bring. I thought a wife and children—a family—was a burden to avoid. After a few years, Madeline started pressuring me to get married, but I always resisted. We even broke up once because I was reluctant to make a commitment. But I loved Madeline and did not want to live without her, so I reluctantly married her and had children, which caused me lifelong resentment at having to support a family.

Hera, the goddess of women, marriage, family, childbirth, and hearth, was heard muttering that Oscar was lucky to get her and that she could have done better.

Madeline and I had three children Megan, Mehal, and Maurice. I am embarrassed to admit this today, but I was not interested in my children. They were unwelcome, so I ignored them. I disliked my oldest daughter Megan because she was rebellious, I repressed the memory of my middle son Mehal after he drowned, and I found my youngest son Maurice curiously affectionate, which I spurned. Madeline, who loved her children and was a doting mother, would say, Oscar, I love you, but you are a fool for not appreciating and loving the most beautiful things you have created. In hindsight I am not sure why Madeline stayed married to such a resentful and shallow person. I am surprised she did not leave me.

Athena then muttered to herself, Me too.

Oscar on His Fear of Death
One reason I was such a shallow person was that I feared the unknown, of which death is the greatest. Dying was an awful prospect for me because I had watched my friend Benas Savickis die in agonizing pain of a heart attack and disappear from the earth forever.

Thanatos then said that a number of psychological things happen to humans when they think like Oscar. The first is they have no horizon, no vision of past and future, and thus become focused on themselves. Second, when they avoid thinking of death, they don't live life fully because they don't value and make the most of the brief life they live. They live a kind of artificial, unauthentic life.

Rhea on Oscar's Unhappiness and Its Consequences
Rhea, the goddess of nature, a kind of wise Spinozian pantheist, said that the greatest psychological consequence of the fear of

death for humans is unhappiness, which makes their lives something to endure rather than to enjoy. There are many reasons for this unhappiness. First, they are unrealistic because their lens of life is skewed; they don't see reality accurately. The second is juvenile emotions. They are driven by base emotions like anger, jealousy, envy, and lust. They never mature and learn to gauge and moderate their emotions. Third, they are prideful, thinking they are the center of the universe and unaware they are really an unimportant speck of sand on a vast ocean beach. The fourth and perhaps primary reason for their unhappiness is their uncontrollable desire. They are never satisfied with what they have; they always want more. For them happiness is what another has, which makes happiness an unfulfillable illusion, like a mirage always appearing somewhere else. Fifth, ironically, their fear of death also leads to bad habits. You would think a person who fears death would take great care of their health to delay it, but what really happens is they ignore the issues of life and death and make habits of whatever makes them feel good now, which are too often bad habits.

As a consequence, humans live unauthentic lives. An unauthentic life means living a lie and being pretentious. It means experiencing a boring and worthless existence without any meaningful goals or achievements. It means to waste your life. Oscar, for example, always told himself that he would do what he really wanted later in life when he had the time, but when he got older, he was too tired and spent to do what he wanted. He had wasted the best part of his young life working only to live with pain during the last and least valuable old part of it. He thus missed enjoying some of the most profound things of life, like love, family, adventure, and learning, and ended up living a dull life that terminated in profound regret.

Panacea, Hygeia, Asclepius, and Iaso on Oscar's Health, the Ways to Die, and Warning Signs

Panacea, goddess of universal remedy and cure, said, Oscar's unauthentic character caused him to take his health for granted. It was easy for him to say he did not care because he avoided thinking about death. But when he got older, his bad habits caught up with him, and it was only then that he began thinking about his impending demise and regretting his bad habits.

The uptight and rude Hygeia, goddess of cleanliness and hygiene, said, Just look how Oscar abused his young body. He should have died long ago. He ate saturated fats and high-cholesterol foods like cheeseburgers and fries every day, and he ate way too much, which is why he is obese.

With that Asclepius, god of health and medicine, said, Hygeia is right. Look how he smoked two packs of cigarettes a day and never exercised except for his Saturday morning basketball games. He also was under constant stress because he had many relationship and work problems that caused chronic anger, which he could never control. He never took time off from life to just unwind.

He could, said Iaso, the goddess of remedy, have taken some measures to control the consequences of his bad habits, but he never did. He took no drugs to control his high blood pressure, which was usually 180–200 over 100–110, or his high cholesterol, which was always over 200. He never had a physical examination by a doctor because he was afraid of what they might say.

Panacea said to Iaso, Oscar's habits and lifestyle are the same causes of most heart attacks; indeed, it is estimated that one-third of people over sixty have high blood pressure. It is no surprise that Oscar was bound to have a heart attack.

Hygeia then rudely interrupted and said that heart attacks are a leading cause of human death, but there are others, like stroke, shock, AIDS, cancer, and Alzheimer's disease. Death by violence, usually from a trauma, physical injury, or wound, is the province of the young. It is the leading cause of death for those under age forty-four in the United States. It is usually due to auto and motorcycle accidents, war, and crime. In such cases 60 percent die within twenty-four hours after injury. The three medical sequences of traumatic dying are immediate, early, and late deaths. Immediate death takes place within minutes of the injury and is always the result of injury to the brain, spinal cord, heart, or a major blood vessel. Early traumatic death occurs within a few hours after the injury and is usually due to brain damage or bleeding. Late death occurs within weeks after the injury and is usually caused by infection and failure of the lungs, kidneys, or liver.

Some other common ways for humans to die include drowning, electrification, and septic shock. Humans suffocate with water when they drown. When lifeless, the human body, which is heavier than water—and the head is the heaviest—sinks headfirst to the bottom and remains in that position for days or weeks. Eventually putrefaction produces enough gas in the tissues to float the corpse to the surface, which is why drowning victims are usually found floating well after they have drowned.

Electrocution, which was once used to execute condemned criminals, makes the nerves go crazy, sending electrical signals to all parts of the body that cause pain, spasms, and the loss of motor function, including the ability to speak. The victim is usually quietly terrified as their body shakes and tenses while it battles the current. All the muscles at once start spasmodically expanding and contracting in response to the current, which is quite painful. Electrocution kills in three ways: by paralyzing the breathing center of the brain, paralyzing the heart, or causing ventricular fibrillation. The latter is the most common way of dying from electrocution. Cardia dysrhythmia occurs because the respiratory muscles become paralyzed due to the current through the head (which often smokes), neck, and brainstem.

Septic shock is the leading cause of death in intensive care units in the United States. Sepsis is blood poisoning, or infection of the blood, or toxins in the blood, and shock is the tissues' reaction to the loss of blood. Septic shock causes numerous organ failures, like kidney failure and gastrointestinal bleeding. If three or more organs are affected, the mortality rate is close to 100 percent.

It was then that Iaso asked Oscar how he felt. At first Oscar said he felt fine, but Iaso pointed out that she had seen him stop playing basketball and gasp for breath a few times. A now worried-looking Oscar said sometimes he did not feel good. Sometimes he got angina, or chest pains, and felt chest tightness, pressure, and discomfort. Iaso asked if that was all, and Oscar said he did get shortness of breath, loss of energy, sometimes numbness, weakness, and coldness in his legs and arms, and occasionally pain his neck, jaw, throat, upper abdomen, and back. Iaso then said to the other gods, These are unmistakable warning signs of heart disease.

Athena nodded to Iaso in agreement and said, It looks like Oscar not only lived a shallow life fearing death but, because he ignored his health, a short one due to heart disease.

CHAPTER 4

Oscar's First Heart Attack

Iaso described to the other gods the amazing human heart. She said, It is an organ that beats more than 2.5 billion times during the average human lifespan, moving about 5.6 liters, or about 1.5 gallons, of blood through the circulatory system. It does this sometimes for as long as one hundred years or even more. But if you have a genetic history of heart disease and, like Oscar, smoke, are fat, are stressed, don't exercise, and ignore your high blood pressure and cholesterol, your heart will rebel, like Oscar's did when he was twenty-eight.

The Human Heart

Asclepius took over the conversation and described the purpose, function, and problems of the heart. First, he said, there are a few medical terms you need to know. Myocardium is the heart muscle, coronary arteries are the heart arteries because they look like a crown, stenosis is an abnormal narrowing, ischemia is lack of blood, and infarction is tissue's reaction and dying due to the lack of blood. The heart is a muscle positioned in the chest behind the sternum, in front of the trachea, esophagus, and aorta, and above the diaphragm. It pumps nutrients and oxygenated blood through arteries to all body organs and tissues. It also regulates fluid balance and body temperature. There are two phases of its cardiac cycle. In the diastole phase, the heart ventricles relax and the heart fills with blood, and in the systole phase, the ventricles contract and pump life-sustaining blood into the arteries.

Oscar's First Heart Attack

When Oscar had his first heart attack at a very young age, a coronary artery of the myocardium had stenosis, which resulted in ischemia and an infarction. A part of Oscar's heart muscle died. Oscar's coronary arteries were becoming bony canals, which made it harder for his heart to pump blood, so his heart muscle thickened and enlarged in order to meet his body's demands. As a result, Oscar suffered chronic fatigue, listlessness, and difficulty breathing due to low cardiac output. Predictably, Oscar occasionally suffered angina pectoris, or excruciating heart pain, and eventually a heart attack—a charley horse of the heart. His heart got strangled when a blood clot in a stenotic area of a coronary artery blocked the blood flow to a portion of his heart muscle, depriving it of oxygen and nutrients. This disrupted his myocardium's normal rhythm and caused squirming ventricular fibrillation as some of Oscar's heart muscle died.

This is called an arrhythmia, a life-threatening electrical problem in Oscar's heart. For most heart attack victims, death begins with ventricular fibrillation and acute pulmonary edema, or excess fluid in the lungs, because the left ventricle is too weak to maintain the blood pressure necessary to sustain life. So victims lose consciousness due to inadequate blood flow to their brain, they suffer kidney failure and uremia—increased nitrogenous urea in the blood—that increases their bodily fluid, and when the blood flow stops, they experience cardiac arrest, which normally brings death within minutes. Human medicine defines clinical death when the heart has stopped, there is no circulation, breathing has ceased, and there is no brain function. Clinical death covers a few minutes; however, resuscitation is possible during this brief period before permanent death.

Fortunately for Oscar, the blockage was in a small coronary artery that supplied blood to a small portion of his heart muscle, so his was a mild, brief heart attack that affected a relatively small portion of his heart muscle and did not cause much permanent heart damage.

Oscar's Description of His Heart Attack
How Oscar Felt It Physically

Asclepius then asked Oscar what a heart attack feels like physically. Oscar was obviously agitated and said, like he had said earlier, You gods, who never die, are holding me here in Limbo where I am awaiting your decision to send me to Heaven or Hell. You are just toying with me, so why should I answer your questions?

Thanatos said, Because we are interested in human death, and if you don't, we will certainly send you to hell!

Oscar blanched and said, It was an awful experience, ten times worse than a dentist drilling on an exposed nerve. I was grocery shopping with Madeline when I got this queasy kind of feeling that could be described as fullness, discomfort, dizzy, and nausea with cold sweats. I had never felt anything like it before. I felt fatigued, clammy, woozy, and chilled. I felt like I was going to throw up, like I had the flu, and had belchy indigestion that felt like heartburn. I was lightheaded and pale and sweating profusely. I told Madeline I did not feel well and, full of fear and anxiety, I sat down, hoping these strange feelings would pass, but it only got worse. It was then I started feeling a weird burning in my chest that quickly became a tight kind of pain that spread to my stomach, neck, and the back of my arms—a heavy pressure was everywhere. Then suddenly I started gasping for breath, and my heart went into a kind of abnormal, racing heartbeat.

It was then that I got this sudden, severe, and viselike crushing pressure in my chest. It felt like an elephant was sitting on me. I doubled up, trying to endure this squeezing, painful pressure that was spreading to other parts of my upper body and hoping that it would go away. I broke out in a cold sweat. I was breathing quickly and shallowly—I felt like I was being asphyxiated because I could not get enough air. After a few minutes, the pain subsided, but it soon returned with a vengeance. All I could think about was the pain, and I hoped that it would go away.

Asclepius said Oscar had been in a very dangerous place. If his ischemia did not let up within ten minutes, the oxygen deficiency may have become irreversible, and some deprived cardiac muscle would have died due to infarction. He needed to quickly get to a hospital because 20 percent of heart attack victims die if not transported to one within the first hour. Even if he made it to the hospital, there is a 50 to 60 percent chance he would have died within an hour of his attack, and if he did survive, he would eventually be claimed by congestive heart disease due to the gradual weakening of his heart's ability to pump.

How Oscar Experienced It Mentally
Asclepius asked Oscar how his attack felt mentally. Oscar winced and said that the mental anguish during his attack was almost worse than the physical pain. He said, Suddenly everything went into slow motion, and there was a gradual change from light to

dark as the lights went out. It felt like I was shrinking and life was draining out of me, which filled me with fear.

Phobos commented that this is the usual human reaction to a heart attack. The victim is terrified that they are going to die, which triggers intense fear and anxiety along with a consuming sense of dread and profound sense of doom.

Oscar reiterated that he remembered during his own heart attack watching this friend Benas Savickis die of a heart attack many years ago, which caused him to panic because he thought this was now happening to him.

Oscar then became uncharacteristically pensive and described some of his semiconscious thoughts. He said, At first, I was terrified at being sucked into a black sack, but as time passed the fear abated, and I found the passage easy, even pleasurable. As I experienced less light and physical sensation, being coaxed into the tunnel felt good. Rather than light becoming dimmer, suddenly it became brighter—it was like leaving the darkness and entering the light. I saw a kaleidoscope of flashing images of my life and the people I knew in it. I saw my parents, grandparents, children, and old friends who I had not seen in years, beckoning me to join them. As my body began to leave me, I felt a profound sense of peace and well-being.

Then suddenly the mirage disappeared, the surgery lights were bright and harsh, the chest pain and mental anguish returned, and I was yanked back into ugly reality. The physical pain and mental anguish were unendurable, and I did not want to return. I yearned to die, but I survived.

The Grim Reaper

Then Euphrosyne, the goddess of good cheer, joy, mirth, and merriment, spoke up and said, Our conversation on human death has been so depressing, it is a pleasure to hear now from our favorite merrymaker, the Grim Reaper.

Grimy, as his friends liked to call him, said, I really don't mind how Chronos, the god of time, has mischaracterized me. You all think of me as a black-clad, brooding apparition that carries a scythe—a kind of bounty hunter dedicated to killing. The truth is I do not kill mortals; rather, I guide their spirits to the next realm. Indeed, my scythe is a mere symbol of reaped souls, like the corn the peasants harvest from the fields. Just look at me, standing in front of you in my Hawaiian shirt, plaid shorts, and sandals—do I look like a daemon? I am rather a jolly and happy-go-lucky fellow who likes to party with Dionysus, drink wine, laugh at a good joke, and chase young women early in the morning with Eros, the god of love and beauty. I also like to pull off pranks. I was the one, along with fellow merrymakers Hades and Chaos, god of nothingness, who snatched Oscar before he died, and bribed Charon, the ferryman who takes souls across the River Styx to Purgatory, to take Oscar to Limbo where he is now. Oscar was not harvested.

Panacea and Iaso on the Remedies

Panacea and Iaso, the gods of remedy, said, You should see how they saved Oscar. He was not harvested because humans have become so clever in ways to thwart nature, avoid death, and prolong life, mostly through their science. Historically, Oscar would have died from his heart attack, but not now.

Oscar had been lying on the supermarket floor, pale and lifeless, with a stopped heart near death. A trained employee turned him on his back, made sure his airways were open, checked his breathing and began cardio pulmonary resuscitation, or CPR. He began compressing his chest thirty times between rescue breaths. Within minutes paramedics arrived and took over. One continued CPR in order to do what the heart and lungs had ceased to do—maintain oxygenated blood to the vital organs, especially the brain. Another gave Oscar a shot of nitroglycerine to open up his arteries while yet another prepared him for the automated external defibrillator, or AED. It had paddles they put on Oscar's chest that sent a regulated electrical current to his heart to get it beating again. Oscar's body jumped a foot or so with each of the three or four shocks, and then his heart began beating. The paramedics quickly put him on a gurney and rushed him to the nearest emergency room. They had done their job, which was to get his heart working again long enough to get to critical cardio hospital care and treatment.

The real work to prevent further damage, repair Oscar's heart, and prevent future attacks began at the hospital. The doctors and nurses flew into their work. They first did an angiography, or imaging technique to see inside Oscar's arteries and heart chambers to find the blockage. The treatment depends on the extent of the blockage. They then gave Oscar hypothermic therapy to reduce his body temperature in order to reduce heart and brain damage. Then they began thrombolytic therapy, which consists of a cocktail of medicines administered through a drip catheter to restore blood flow to the heart through the coronary arteries. Some of these medicines included antiplatelet agents (to prevent blood clots), an angiotensin (to expand blood vessels), a beta blocker (to lower blood pressure), a vasodilator (to relax blood vessels), an antiplatelet agent like warfarin, or rat poison (to prevent blood clotting), and a fibrinolytic drug (to restore blood flow). Oscar became a living pharmacy.

They next whisked Oscar into surgery because they knew that if surgical procedures were not done within three hours of the attack, Oscar's heart could be permanently damaged beyond repair. There were are a variety of surgical options for Oscar. Some included angioplasty (where a balloon is inflated at the blockage), laser angioplasty (where a catheter with a laser tip opens blocked arteries), atherectomy (where a catheter with a rotating shaver tip cuts plaque away from the artery wall), and ultimately a heart transplant (where a diseased heart is replaced by one donated by a healthy human).

The doctors decided that the treatment for Oscar was a stent. They inserted a long, thin catheter into a blood vessel and, with the help of imaging dye, guided it to the blocked coronary artery. Once there they inserted an expandable metal mesh tube into the blocked part of the artery and expanded it to prop it open. With that Oscar's chest pains immediately stopped, to Oscar's great relief.

When Oscar was released from the hospital, the cardiac physician who had treated him told a now humble Oscar, There are some hereditary reasons for your heart attack, but it was caused mostly by your bad habits. He said, Stop smoking, lose weight, exercise, and take your medicines. He told Oscar he needed to keep his blood pressure under 130/90, which meant taking his blood pressure pills, atenolol and olmesartan, watching what he eats, and keeping his cholesterol well under 200 with atorvastatin, keeping his blood thinned with 81 mg. aspirin, and to take digitalis if needed to increase the force of his heart's contractions.

Asclepius again took over the conversation and asked Oscar what he thought about his first heart attack. Oscar, still irritated at being held in Limbo, said he had mixed feelings. He said, On one hand I am angry, because it was you gods who gave me this heart attack and made ischemic heart disease the leading cause of death in industrialized nations of the world. But on the other I am grateful that the pain is over and I did not die after my first heart attack. I felt like a million pounds had been lifted off my chest.

Asclepius said, You were very lucky, Oscar, because you survived your heart attack with minimal damage, although you probably experienced some angina pectoris, or chest pain, later in life.

Oscar, who had spent days in fear and trembling that he would die at age twenty-eight, became uncharacteristically contemplative about the nature of death because he had come so close to it. He told the doctor he was right. I will change my habits and take better care of my health.

The Grim Reaper was heard saying he doubted it and that he expected to harvest Oscar soon.

CHAPTER 5

The Nature of Death

A FTER HIS FIRST HEART ATTACK, OSCAR LIVED IN FEAR OF DYING. For the first time in his life, he had felt tremendous pain that could kill him. He became acutely aware that someday it most likely would, which was an alarming thought. He also thought about how so many had died before him and how routine it was for people to die. This caused the young Oscar to think about the circumstances of his existence—his usually placid mind began to contemplate the nature of death. He first thought was that the gods were to blame for letting him suffer and die, but eventually he realized it was nature that was so hostile to his life. He realized how indifferent nature was to his welfare. He thought how nature had little regard for his mind, his life, and his death, which made him feel small, fragile, and ephemeral. Indeed, he thought, after I die, nature will not even be aware I was here.

The Nature of Death
Oscar thought about his ancestors and their views on death. Some thought death is not the end of existence and there is an afterlife,

and others believed at death we become nothing, just worm food. He then wondered when and how his death might happen and winced at the pain another heart attack could bring. He asked himself what he feared most—the pain of dying or, if there is no afterlife, becoming nonexistent?

Then Rhea, the goddess of nature and a philosopher, told Oscar that the thoughts he was having about death were timeless. They are the same questions humans have been asking for eons. She said, The simplest explanation I can give you is to compare death with sleep.

This comment excited Hypnos, who said death is just like sleeping without the dreams, having to get up to pee, and waking up. You all have experienced the comatose state of sleep, totally unaware of the surrounding reality, which state is just like death. But with sleep you gradually awaken and integrate yourself into that surrounding reality, and death is when you don't—you remain comatose.

Irritated at being interrupted, Rhea said, Thanks, Hypnos, but death is more than a sleep analogy. To understand it, we must first define it.

But defining death is not so easy. Some say it occurs when vital biologic functions, like respiration and circulation, cease; others say that a person is dead when the cerebellum dies; still others say that death is the permanent and functional death of the brain stem. In some advanced Western nations, an individual is dead when either there is an irreversible cessation of circulatory and respiratory functions or there is an irreversible cessation of all functions of the entire brain, including the brain stem. One simple final definition says a person is dead when they are no longer existent.

But there are numerous problems with these definitions. Zygotes and embryos can be frozen, like seeds and spores, and have no biologic functions during that time, but they can still become alive. They are not alive, but they also are not dead. Further, imagine a device that repairs corpses that have not decomposed beyond repair. It could move molecules back to where they were before death and restart the vital processes—it could restore life to people who have died. A person who has lost the use of their brain and brain stem could be brought back to life. Also, consider an amoeba's ability to split and continue to exist. The original amoeba is gone, but it lives on in two new ones; it has and has not ceased to exist. I should also mention some think one must have lived in the past in order to be dead today, but consider a seed. It did not live in the past, but it can live in the future.

So there is difficulty defining death, but it gets more complicated when trying to describe what it is, or its nature. There seem to be only two possibilities, which were delineated and advocated by Oscar's ancestors: a dead person goes out of existence, or a dead person goes somewhere else.

It was here that Nemesis, the malevolent goddess of retribution and vengeance, spoke up and said, You all make more of death than it is. With that she sent a thunderbolt through her fingers at a mouse scurrying across the room, who immediately went into spasms, shuddered, and died. There, shouted Nemesis, that is death.

Rhea, who thought the demonstration was gross but knew Nemesis was a difficult goddess who disliked everyone, said, Nemesis has demonstrated the view of Oscar's practical philosopher ancestors. They called it *materialism*, which means living things are material first. The ancient philosopher Lucretius made this point with his statement that nothing comes from nothing. A living thing comes from material; it does not just appear out of nowhere. This means that when living things die, they return to the material from which they arose; the individual does not survive death. Death is the cessation of physical and chemical activity when the body returns to inert matter—or the elements of the earth, like carbon—from which it came. The body ceases to function and decays, the mind stops thinking and crumbles, the heart stops beating, the lungs stop breathing, and the body gradually becomes worm food. There is no continuing consciousness, there is no elsewhere or somewhere else, because the brain needed oxygenated blood to think, which has ceased. Life responds to stimuli and involves growth, reproduction, adaptability, and metabolism, but when it dies, it does not respond to stimuli. It disintegrates rather than grows, it cannot reproduce, it no longer adapts, and its metabolism has ceased to function. Death is the ending of living.

I understand how much this view of death bothers some people, but that is due to their emotional reaction to becoming nothing; it has nothing to do with what really happens. To support this view of death, I will discuss materialism later, including the illuminating story of Phineas Gage, but for now consider how inevitable and natural it is for a living body to wear out and return to the elements. Indeed, this materialistic view has historically been attractive to many human philosophers.

Your ancient Stoic philosophers Cicero, Epictetus, and Marcus Aurelius advocated this practical materialistic view of life and death. Cicero wrote, *Die when nature says—those were the terms of the loan.* Epictetus wrote, *You are a soul carrying a corpse, your poor body is not your own—it is to nature a corpse,* and *If corn had sense, would it wish not to be reaped-likewise, man should not curse death—it is natural.* Roman emperor and last of the Stoic philosophers Marcus Aurelius wrote that *death is just a function of nature, and only children fear nature's function; an educated attitude toward death does not find it superficial or disdainful, rather, simply awaiting it is one of the functions of nature and to remember, that whether it is you or someone else, it won't be long before you'll be dead and it won't be long before your name won't even be left [so] do not act [as if you are] going to live ten thousand years.*

Then Elpis, goddess of hope, rose and said, Not everyone is a materialistic stoic. Virtually all faith-based beliefs, like Oscar's religious ancestors, have advocated a religious or metaphysical explanation in which humans go somewhere else when they die. They have postulated heavens and hells, Greek Empyrean fields for brave warriors, and reincarnation, and they cite near-death experiences, or NDEs, to support their claims. These faiths are humans' only hope for a life after death.

Certainly, some humans deride these beliefs as wishful and emotional thinking—ideas that come from those that fear death. But there are some powerful arguments for these beliefs. First, the skeptics cannot disprove that an afterlife exists; indeed, their denial of an afterlife is a faith-based belief itself! Second, the rational science they so often cite itself postulates places beyond time and space, hidden dimensions, and multiple realms and universes, as well as a Big Bang theory that says the universe had a beginning. These are no different than religion's metaphysical ideas. These skeptics are unable to prove religions' views wrong, and it seems to me, it is better to have hope and believe. Belief makes humans happier because they then accept death with serenity. Oh yes, one last point that supports faith-based death views: thousands of people have had near-death experiences, with similar stories of a place full of light, a benevolent God, and peaceful tranquility. How can this be if there is no afterlife? I will explain these near-death experiences later.

Rhea thanked Elpis for her explanation but said she was skeptical of her claims. She asked how religion knows there is an afterlife. Indeed, the burden of proof is on religion to prove its point, because it is claiming knowledge of something. It would seem that a more realistic explanation would be that the faithful are postulating something that sounds better than death and decay because it makes people feel good. It is an idea that makes humans more than stuff, which appeals to their emotions. Further, Rhea added, who would want to live forever? It would be like never getting permission to leave the party, thus being forced to do the same monotonous things over and over for eternity. What a dreadful thought!

Humans Cannot Know Death

I am also skeptical, Rhea continued, that humans will ever understand the nature of death. How can they possibly conceive of their nonexistence when they look at it from inside? They have no outside point of observation or reference and thus no ability to put death in perspective. It would be like trying to explain time when all they can do is describe its effects and not itself.

Further, their senses are unable to experience annihilation or unconsciousness. With death they can only describe the consequences of nothingness but not nothingness itself. They cannot understand it because death has, like art, no essence to comprehend and define. Humans understand from experience, but with death they have no experience to draw on. They don't even know how to frame the questions to ask about it—questions about what it is, what its nature is, why it happens, and if it has any meaning. It is all incomprehensible to them.

Think about it: millions of humans have died, but none have returned to describe what death is like. You would think a human that could return would want to, but none have. Sure, some of their psychics and people with near-death experiences claim to talk to the dead or to have died and returned, but have they? I am skeptical and inclined to think these assertions are either charlatan or mistaken. The state of death is not something to be explained, rather just something that happens.

But why does it matter that humans cannot know what death is? All their questions just present an impenetrable dilemma that they respond to with wrong answers.

Know Death Only When You Know Life

The truth is death is an intensely private event that, when humans think about it, can be conceived only in relation to life and within a personal conversation with themselves.

At this point, Aether, the god of light and the atmosphere—an often absent-minded god—said, Rhea, you make vague and often incomprehensible points. I find it hard to understand you.

Rhea, who was heard complaining in a mumble that she had to deal with idiot gods like Elpis and Aether, said, Let me try to be clearer. Humans can only know death when they know life. They can only contemplate it when they are living, or, put another way, nonexistent humans do not contemplate death. What this means is that before humans can contemplate death, they have to know what it means to live, which itself is no easy answer. Certainly, they can describe life as certain vital processes, like a beating heart and breathing lungs, that are not present in death, but it is far more complicated than that.

A brilliant human, Alan Turing, once conceived of a test for being alive. He posited putting an isolated human in one room with a microphone, and a computer that had all the attributes of a human in another. Then would each be asked questions, and if the questioner could not discern which was a machine and which a human, Turing would infer that a machine that exhibited intelligent behavior equivalent to a human must be human. If you cannot tell the difference between a human and a machine, which does not experience death, how can you describe death to a human in a way that makes it the opposite of life?

Death Is a Conversation with Oneself

The point is that when humans contemplate death, they are really carrying on an intensely private conversation with themselves. In normal human conversation, people usually exchange useful information about the weather, politics, or themselves. But with death there is no genuinely true information to exchange, which means each human is really talking with themselves about a topic they don't understand. Nobody goes with them when they die, so they have nobody to discuss it with but themselves. Certainly, they can exchange consequential information on death, like a doctor who can describe how someone died due to a ski accident, but they cannot convey information about the nature of death itself because they don't know.

Is Death a Blessing or a Curse?

After thinking awhile about what had been said about death, a confused Oscar asked the goddess Metis, goddess of wisdom, whether death is a blessing or a curse.

Metis was startled to be asked a question because she was so often ignored, unlike Athena, the other goddess of wisdom. Metis was a follower of Socrates and believed his admonition that wisdom is knowing that you do not know, which often made her look like a brilliant mathematician who always got the wrong answer. Naturally, she first said she was not sure if death is a blessing or curse, but she would discuss both sides and perhaps make a decision based on that.

She said, This is a natural question about death humans ask. The best way to begin is to ask if death harms you. On the surface the answer would appear to be yes, because death not only annihilates you, Oscar, but also deprives you of future benefits. But think a little: annihilation may not be so bad for many people, and death could save you from having to experience bad things in the future. It seems it could go either way. Let us examine whether death harms people—whether it is a blessing or curse.

A Blessing

I have already mentioned how death could save you from future harms, but the ancient philosopher Epicurus carried that point even further. He pointed out that when you are dead, there is nobody to harm. Our corpse burned does not harm us, and it has no effect on you when you are alive because it has not yet occurred. Death can only harm you while it occurs, which it sometimes does, but not before or after dying. Further, one motivation or reason to be interested in living is desire—wanting things like love, a family, and children. But as you age, most of these desires have been fulfilled or abandoned. Many advanced in age have achieved their goals, so death cannot thwart their desires. With the loss of desire and concomitant loss of motivation to live, death ceases to be objectionable to them. Indeed, when you are dead, there is nothing more to look forward to.

Death also brings a few practical benefits. It releases you from all worldly cares, like relationship problems, money, and the health of your body. How wonderful to be free forever from these hindrances that torment so many when alive. Further, imagine what your life would be like if you could live forever. It would be a grinding and utterly boring stale routine with no novelty.

Also, Oscar, I have heard you say that you are afraid of becoming nothing after death. Why would you think that? The philosopher

Lucretius, who was a follower of Epicurus, pointed out that you were nothing before you were born and you don't fear that, so why are you afraid of the same state after you die? To make the point clearer, imagine a futuristic machine that could dismantle and rebuild you after nonexistence, a machine that could move you in and out of existence like a bear hibernating in the winter. Would you be upset by the intervening gaps of nonexistence? It seems more likely you would come to enjoy the occasional breaks from life. At a minimum, if there is an afterlife and you have been good, you could go to Heaven and live in eternal bliss.

So it seems to me death and nonexistence do not harm you, but rather often bring a good thing to a necessary close, which makes them harmful only if you could survive them.

A Curse

Then Metis turned to Oscar and said, I know, because of your heart attack, you have come to think of death as a curse. You find the thought of death making your body a corpse repugnant, which makes death for you an evil event. Well, in some respects you are right.

I mentioned earlier that the harm theory could go either way, and it could harm you if it deprived you of certain future benefits. Death could prevent you from enjoying years of pleasant activities. Who knows, you could win a million dollars in the lottery, or take up auto racing and come in second in the Indianapolis 500, or experience the joy of many grandchildren. Death would take all this away, causing you harm. If you are young and healthy, a premature death due to war, an auto accident, or being murdered would also be a harm because it took your future benefits and was probably painful.

I mentioned earlier how desires enliven you and make you want to live fully, which a premature death thwarts—it thwarts your desires. Similarly, you have active forward-looking goals. You make and pursue plans for the future because it can be influenced (you don't make plans for the past because it cannot be changed). You make these plans to enhance the pleasures of your life. But like desires, death takes away this ability to plan, which makes death a harm with no future to plan.

Finally, death is a harm to those who want to continue to live, to those who have aspirations to live well, and to those who die in excruciating pain. Being tortured, shot in war, or suffocating from lung cancer are harms to those unfortunate souls. I should also mention, as I did for death as a blessing, that if there is an afterlife and you have been bad, then you could spend eternity suffering in Hell.

After more pondering, Metis then said to Oscar that she thought death was a blessing for three reasons. First, those who died prematurely and whose desires, goals, and future benefits had been thwarted don't know it after they die. Second, death is natural, and how can something natural be called a curse? It just is. Third, you have no choice. You will die, and there is nothing you can do about it. Fretting is a waste of time. It is best to accept it and move on.

Which leads to the idea that death is how you think about it. A rock is a rock—it only changes when you begin calling it a flower. The world is as you make, it so realize that once you are dead, death itself is neither pleasant nor unpleasant because there is no longer a you to experience it. Ultimately, death has no positive or negative value because a dead person cannot be benefited or harmed. So, Oscar, you should not think of death with sorrow or terror; rather, focus your mind on your life and not your death.

Ways Humans Die

Then Hygeia reminded Oscar that she had explained some of the ways humans die earlier, and now she wanted to describe another:

shock. She said, I am not talking about electrical shock, but rather the lack of blood supply. There are many causes of shock, but the main ones are uncontrolled bleeding, severe burns, and spinal injury. There are numerous types of shock, but the most common is distributive shock, of which septic shock is a common cause of death. Shock kills by causing a drop in blood pressure, which reduces the flow of oxygen and nutrients to your vital organs, such as the brain, heart, and lungs, so they stop working.

Then Hygeia said, Rather than describe the symptoms of shock, let me show it to you in person. There is always a war going on with you humans, so let me show you a nineteen-year-old young man who has just been shot in Afghanistan. Hygeia then created a life-hologram of a real event happening: a battlefield in the American war with Afghanistan. She said, Here is the young man on the ground in anguish and gushing blood. This horrified Oscar. The bullet severed his aorta, so mercifully he will die quickly. His first reaction on being shot was anxiety, confusion, and nausea, and his skin quickly became cold, sweaty, and pale. Within twenty seconds or, so he began to breath irregularly, sweated profusely, got dizzy, and had dilated, lackluster eyes. Finally, his pulse became rapid, he shivered violently, and because he had lost half of his blood, his heart stopped beating and he died. When a major vessel like the aorta is lacerated, the process of death takes less than a minute. This is shock, and left untreated it is usually fatal.

Then Athena, in her wisdom, spoke up and thanked Hygeia and Metis for their comments. She said to Oscar, It is true that much of death is how you think about it, so next let us describe various human attitudes toward death and how some might be replaced with better ones.

CHAPTER 6
Philosophy and Death

T HE GODS HAD DISCUSSED THE NATURE OF DEATH, AND IN particular whether it is a blessing or curse, which made Oscar feel small and insignificant. After his first heart attack, he had become more cynical towards life, began to see how pointless trying to live was, and wondered if he should just disappear into that black sack like his friend Benas Savickis. He kept asking himself if life was worth it. But he also thought he had much to experience, which could involve adventures and excitements, so why leave so soon? Why not make the most of the rest of my life?

Athena then, like Rhea before her, said that Oscar's thoughts are typical of humans who have contemplated life and death. She said to Oscar that the most important thing about your death is your attitude toward it when you are alive. To help us understand why, I have asked Apollo, the god of sun and light who is prescient, Hygeia, goddess of health and longevity, and Rhea because she knows philosophy, to join us.

Oscar's Ill Health and Fear of Death

Oscar said he looked forward to the discussion because his attitude toward death was becoming fatalistic and his zest for living was waning. Hygeia reminded Oscar that after his heart attack, he had resolved to change his habits. She said, You were successful for a while, but lately you have been backsliding. You stopped exercising, gained weight, started smoking again, and are not taking your medicines on a regular basis. I have noticed your occasional attacks of angina and shortness of breath, which are ominous warning signs. She said, You are so typical of humans. You can be resolute when in danger, but when the danger abates, you quickly slip back into your old ways.

Then Apollo started talking to Oscar, which intimidated him because he was being spoken to by the awesome god of sun and light. Apollo said, Hygeia is right, and if you don't mend your ways, you will die from another heart attack, or possibly congestive heart disease. As your symptoms get gradually worse, you will come to the realization that you are going to die. I will show you the destructive attitudes toward death you will experience when you come to that realization.

Elisabeth Kubler-Ross, a wise human, described the five stages of grief you will experience as you die. The first is denial (a real attitude and not a river in Egypt), where you will live in disbelief and cling to some false preferable reality. However, denial will not make you feel better, so you will get angry—the second stage. Your anger will become frustration, and you will begin selfishly asking, Why me? This will lead to your third stage, bargaining, in which you will jejunely attempt to negotiate with fate. You will promise to reform your lifestyle and seek compromises in order to avoid grief. When you finally come to understand that you cannot bargain with fate, you will experience stage four, depression. You will despair of knowing reality and become silent, isolate yourself, and refuse all visitors, and spend much time mourning in silence. This will last for a while, but what always changes it is the skeptical attitude that naturally arises and says, Why bother, because I am going to die soon? Why go on? This leads to the fifth and final stage, acceptance. You will accept your mortality and inevitable fate.

Oscar looked long and hard at Apollo and said, You scare me. I may well go through the torture you describe in the future, but I would rather not think about it now.

Wisdom and Death

But Oscar, Athena scolded, you must think about your death now if you want to live a full life. There are two attitudes you can take towards your death. Let me describe the destructive one first.

You can think in abstract terms, where death always happens to others. You can think death is arbitrary and senseless and thus does not deserve consideration. You can think that you are too young to die and are thus being robbed of life. You can think you do not deserve death because you have lived life rightly. And finally you could become angry with others, especially your family, because they are pretending you are not sick and will survive you. With these kinds of thoughts, you are living in denial because you know it will happen to you. Your death is real and not arbitrary and sense-less. Selfishly thinking that death robs you ignores the realities of dying young and only leads to envy for the healthy. Living life rightly does not guarantee longevity, and getting angry with others is like throwing a tomato at an oncoming freight train to stop it.

On the other hand, you can adopt constructive, salubrious attitudes. These are not platitudes, but rather palatable explana-tions toward death that help you accept it, thus making you feel less alone. Reflect on your blessings and the good things life has brought you, like family and friends. Think about the goals and projects you have now and not about doing something for the last time. Rather than fight the necessity of death, will it upon yourself so it is not forced. Remind yourself of the fragility of life in contrast to the infinity of time and how the world will naturally continue after you are gone. Remember what Marcus Aurelius once wrote: *Soon there will be others mourning the man who buries you.* Remember, it is your duty to die. Certainly, there is the duty to live if others depend on you, but there is also a duty to die in order to let them inherit the world.

Consider what Derek Parfitsaid about living: if we were able to view past and future events equally, then we would enjoy looking either backwards or forwards over our lives. Being at the end of our lives would be more like being at the beginning, because at any point during our lives, we would enjoy the view. The consequence would be that we would be less depressed by aging and the approach of death. Also, remember our oft-repeated comment that you being nothing is the rule and you living is the exception. Only your imagination makes you think living is the rule, so rein in your imagination.

Other explanations of death seem designed to diminish its gravity. Mark Twain always envied the dead, Captain Hook, in *Peter Pan*, thought death was the only great adventure left to him, and Plato in the *Timaeus* described death as being *loosened from bonds, and fly[ing] away with joy.* Also, remember that healthy-minded people think it is unnatural to fear death because it is the natural consequence of life.

Finally Athena said, Oscar, you need to connect with the people you love and respect when you are approaching death.

This caused Oscar to blanch and say he had heard his relations and coworkers talk about him after his death, each being inconvenienced and hopeful of gain from his passing.

Startled, Athena asked how Oscar knew this, and he said, Hades, Chios, and Grimy arranged for me to hear my friends and relations comments after I "died."

Athena said, Well, they should not have done that, but what you heard was true: most people care little for you. However, recall how little Luke O'Sullivan, the poor young messenger boy in your office, who was working to improve his life, revered you, and how your son Maurice always loved you, even though you ignored him.

This caused Oscar to pause and think deeply for a long time.

Athena then told Oscar, There are three more constructive ways to look at death worth repeating. First, your death is inevitable, so you might as well accept it and live your life to its fullest today. Second, if you lived a thousand years, you would be utterly bored because you will have seen the same things over and over. And third, you have no reason to fear becoming nothing because that is what you were originally, and you don't fear that. Shakespeare wrote that *our little life / Is rounded with a sleep*, and you mostly sleep.

Philosophy and Death

A significant source of wise insights on death, continued Athena, comes from your philosophers, who have been thinking and commenting on it for years. Your ancient Epicureans, led by Epicurus, believed that you should be indifferent to death because it cannot be sensed. For them, fearing something that cannot be experienced was nonsense. Your Stoics had much to say on death. Cicero wrote that *the whole life of the philosopher is preparation for death* and that *a foretaste of the blessing of death: to die with a song of rapture.* Epictetus and Aurelius proposed that universal mechanistic laws governing all natural phenomena determined your fate, including death. They reasoned that resistance to death is foolish because everything is determined. Epictetus wrote that we should think *it is now time for the material from which [we are] composed to be restored again to whence it came,* which is not a terrible thought, and that *we cannot escape death, but we can escape the dread of it.* Marcus Aurelius wrote that *you may leave this life at any moment; keep this possibility in your mind in all that you say or think,* that *both the longest lived and earliest to die suffer the same loss, the present,* and *if this is all he has, he cannot lose what he does not have,* that *you should always look on human life as cheap,* and that *death is relief from…the senses, impulse, the analytical mind and the flesh.*

Some of your more recent thinkers, like Descartes, attempted to understand being rationally. Descartes thought a human was two things, a mind and a body, and this dualism enabled many to surmise that only your body dies, not your mind or soul, which many thought was immortal. It was a flawed but reasoned way to escape death. Gustave Flaubert wrote that *death holds no terrors for a philosopher.* Death comes easier to those who have given it the most thought, like a philosopher. Because they have envisioned themselves dead, they are prepared for its imminence. They have come to accept it and thus die resigned, reconciled, and tranquil. They know that death is a natural part of life. Michel de Montaigne wrote that *our death is part of the order of the universe; it is the condition of our creation,* and Simone de Beauvoir wrote in her autobiography, *My death interrupts my life only when I die, and that only from the point of view of others. Death does not exist for me while I am alive; my project goes right through it without meeting any obstacles.*

A few of your more recent philosophers' observations have been more perspicuous. Martin Heidegger described death as a necessary condition of life. For him, angst in life is caused by not admitting to ourselves that we are human beings who die.

Viewing death as a necessary condition of life is healing and allows us to live a stronger and more vivacious life. Finally, the philosopher George Santayana wrote, *Let us make the best of that moment of wakefulness, after all, there is no cure for birth and death save to enjoy the interval.*

Then Metis, the goddess of wisdom, said, Athena you have described some wise views on death well, but you have not shown Oscar how these attitudes toward death have changed over time. In ancient times ignorance was the rule, so mysterious imaginary gods were conceived, like us, in order to explain phenomena. In the Middle Ages, a religion reigned in which a benevolent God arranged for Heaven in order to make the specter of death less fearsome. The Renaissance ushered in rationality, which led to modern science and humans' incredible ability to manipulate death. Their medicine now can prolong life, repair body damage, defeat diseases, create life, and resuscitate the dead—abilities that were unheard of until recently.

Also, humans' attitude toward death has changed over time. Reason has overcome superstition, science has supplanted religion, most believe in free will rather than fate, and existentialism has challenged Aristotle's teleological purpose. For many, the Empyrean fields and Hell have been replaced by Spinoza's pantheism. Finally, there is one wise message taught by the ancient Stoics that has not changed: you are what you think, which you can use to control your fear of death.

Would You Want to Live Forever?

The goddess Rhea then said, After hearing all this, there are two questions to ask you, Oscar Uzgalis. These important questions have already been discussed and will be expanded on later; they are: would you want to live forever, and when should you die?

Regarding the first question, it is true that to live long you must choose the right mother and father, but consider that a good life does not depend on your length of days, but rather in the use of your time. A person may have lived long but lived little. But more importantly, it seems clear that the worst thing that could happen to you is to be told you will live forever. Earlier, I likened life to going to a party using famous cynical atheist Christopher Hitchens's example. Hitchens derogatorily described a god he called "the boss" who determines your length of life, or stay at the party of life. He can do one of four things to you: The first is to not invite you to the party, which is a slight for some but attractive to others who would prefer not to endure life's hardships. The second is when the party ends, he makes you leave, which is not so onerous. The third is when the party continues and you leave voluntarily, an alternative that is also not so bad. But the fourth choice is when the party continues and the boss tells you that you cannot leave—you are doomed to party for eternity. This really bothers humans, which makes conspicuous the empty desire for immortality.

Die in Your Own Era

The second question is, when should you die? For now, let me say it is best to die in your own era. You are allotted only so much time to live, and if you exceed it, you are encroaching on others' time. And when your family and friends are gone and your time has passed, so you should also.

Ways Humans Die

At this point Asclepius took over the conversation and said, We have described the various ways humans die, and one common one is by a stroke. A stroke is when the blood supply to part of the brain is interrupted or reduced, preventing brain tissue from getting oxygen and nutrients. The catastrophic result is that brain cells die within minutes. Strokes are the fifth leading cause of death and disability in the United States, killing more than 150,000 Americans each year.

There are numerous warning signs of a stroke. These include the sudden onset of weakness or numbness on one side of the body, sudden speech difficulty or confusion, sudden difficulty seeing in one or both eyes, sudden onset of dizziness, trouble walking or loss of balance, sudden severe headache with no known cause, the face drooping, and arm weakness. When these symptoms occur, it is a medical emergency. Prompt treatment is crucial for survival. Without medical attention, the disrupted blood supply to the brain quickly kills brain cells that control the body's automatic life support systems, like breathing and heartbeat, which brings death. Most people die within six months of a major stroke.

Worried-looking Oscar said that he felt bombarded by so much information that he was frightened, confused, and still afraid of death. He said he was particularly worried about Hygeia and Apollo's comments that he would not live much longer.

So Hygeia asked, Then why not do something about it?

CHAPTER 7
Oscar's Second Heart Attack

Hygeia, obviously irritated by Oscar's lack of resolve, told him that most people fear death, which is quite normal but unnecessary. She told him that he seemed to be suffering from thanatophobia, or the intense, often irrational, anxious fear of death. Death consumes your thoughts, she said, which in your case may not be irrational because you had a heart attack at the young age of twenty-eight. The statistics show that about one in five people who have had a heart attack will be readmitted to the hospital for a second one within five years.

But this assumes they did not change their bad habits, which you did for a while, and I was impressed. You ate less, stopped eating foods saturated in fats and cholesterol, lost weight, exercised regularly, quit smoking, reduced your stress, monitored your blood pressure, and took your medications for blood pressure, cholesterol, and aspirin to thin your blood. You also had regular physical exams to check your health. With these life changes, people rarely have a second heart attack, but you gradually quit this healthy regimen because you forgot how painful your heart attack was. So it is very likely you will have a second heart attack at thirty-two, which increases your chances of dying. Indeed, I see that Grimy has arrived, which is not a good omen.

This sent shivers down Oscar's spine.

Grimy, as his usual jocular self and obviously inebriated, entered with a red face and a big smile. He said he needed to make this harvest quick because he wanted to return to Dionysus's party. He had been making good time with Aphrodite. Hygeia told Grimy that Oscar had quit his healthy ways and thus was angling for a second heart attack. Grimy said, Well, let's see what happens.

Oscar's Second Heart Attack

Sure enough, the next day when Oscar was mowing his lawn, he felt weak and nauseous, so he sat down. He recognized the early symptoms of a heart attack and was terrified.

How Oscar Felt Physically

Hygeia asked him what happened, and he said he was sure that he was going to die because he recognized the same symptoms of his first heart attack. He said, You already described two of them, angina and shortness of breath, but there were other unmistakable symptoms, including dizziness, nausea, and lightheadedness. I happened to see my reflection in a window, and I was pale and sweating profusely.

Shortly I began getting thrombosis, or heart spasms, and ventricular fibrillation. My heartbeat became abnormal and irregular, and my heart raced. It was then that the worst hit me—the vicelike crushing pressure on my chest that buckled me over and had me writhing on the ground in excruciating pain. I had forgotten how painful a heart attack is. My heart was starving for oxygen and my body for oxygenated blood. I lay there for a while in a quasi-comatose state until Madeline found me and called an ambulance that rushed me to the nearest hospital emergency room.

How Oscar Felt Mentally

Hygeia, Panacea, Iaso, and Grimy listened to Oscar's description of his second heart attack with interest. Iaso then asked Oscar what he was thinking.

Oscar paused and said, as he had told them earlier, he knew this was a heart attack and was terrified that it would be the one to kill him. He said, How can I possibly describe what I was thinking and feeling at the time? I suppose it would be like a condemned person's thoughts a few minutes before they are executed. They don't think much because they are numb with fear. Indeed, there is not much for them to think about, because they will be dead shortly with no thoughts and no future. It's no use their thinking about other people, of their future plans or their life problems, because they will disappear. These all depended on their being alive to experience them. Likewise, I experienced the same mental anguish, intense fear, and anxiety, along with a consuming sense of dread, like my first heart attack. The only difference was an increased sense of doom because, without making those life changes mentioned earlier, I knew few survive their second heart attack.

Oscar Describes Dying

Panacea then asked Oscar what happened at the hospital. Oscar said, They did most of the same things they did for my first heart attack, including an angiography, and the same cocktail of medicines to restore blood flow to my heart: antiplatelet agents, an angiotensin, a beta blocker, a vasodilator, warfarin, and a fibrinolytic drug. But even with that, my heart stopped a couple of times and the emergency room doctors had to use electrical paddles to restart it. I almost died, and I experienced the realistic vision of being sucked into a black sack just like my first attack.

Then Oscar became quiet, obviously pondering something. After a while he said he thought his anticipation of death, or when he was in pain worrying about dying, was actually worse than dying itself. He said the morbid truth is, he actually began looking forward to dying. He said he again saw his parents, grandparents, and old friends with smiling faces waving for him to join them. He wanted to go, and the passage to death again felt easy, even pleasurable. But then, just like the last time, he was rudely yanked back into bright lights and ugly reality.

Modern Medicine Saves Oscar

Fortunately for Oscar, like the first one, this was a mild heart attack. The same small coronary artery had become blocked again and choked off oxygenated blood to a part of his heart. The medicine that reduces plaque buildup in the stent they had inserted after his first attack had worn away, and the stent had become encrusted. The surgeons decided Oscar needed triple bypass surgery. Coronary artery bypass graft surgery, or CABG (pronounced cabbage), is when a blood vessel is taken from the chest, leg, or arm and attached or grafted to the coronary artery, which lets blood bypass the narrowed or blocked artery. It treats blocked heart arteries by creating new passages for blood to flow to the heart muscle.

Oscar spent hours in the operating room while a surgeon cut down the midline of his chest and through the breastbone to reach the heart. Another surgeon harvested a blood vessel from his leg to graft to his heart, bypassing the blockage. This improved the blood flow to his heart and saved him from death, but ominously a little more of his precious heart muscle had died.

Oscar Contemplates Suicide

After Oscar returned home, he went into a deep depression. He was distraught that his heart was permanently damaged and would never be completely healthy. He felt his life was less vital, he tired easily, and he had occasional bouts of angina and shortness of breath. Because of this Oscar began contemplating suicide.

Observing Oscar's thinking, Thanatos said, This is a common human reaction to ill health. Worldwide, over 700,000 people die by suicide each year, mostly in low and middle-income countries. It is the fourth leading cause of death in fifteen- to nineteen-year-olds and the highest rate of death for elderly males facing illness, loneliness, and depression. Further, in the United States, it is a leading cause of death (it was the eleventh cause of death in 2007) with more than 45,000 Americans committing it each year and hundreds of thousands that attempt it but fail.

In the United States, the highest rate of suicide deaths are elderly people who have undiagnosed or untreated depression, often due to traumas like loss of a spouse or chronic illness; those experiencing conflict, disaster, violence, abuse, or isolation; people who are part of vulnerable groups experiencing discrimination, such as refugees and migrants, indigenous peoples, LGBTI (lesbian, gay, bisexual, transgender, and intersex), and prisoners.

Globally, the three ways most people commit suicide are by hanging, firearm, and ingestion of pesticide. The latter, whish is a type of poisoning, is a particularly gruesome way to die. The human body has thousands of chemical processes that keep it alive, which poison interferes with in many ways. Some inhibit the production of energy, some disrupt communication between nerve cells, and others disrupt the muscles' ability to move, often causing suffocation. Cyanide, for example, attacks the enzyme that metabolizes sugar in the mitochondria that produce, in a complicated way, oxygen and ultimately energy. Cyanide disrupts the enzyme cells in the body, which die because they can no longer use oxygen. Of all the ways to be poisoned, pesticide poisoning is one of the worst, and it's a common way in undeveloped countries because pesticide is usually available.

Nervous Oscar said that his first love in life, a beautiful young fifteen-year-old girl named Ugne who lived on a farm near him in Lithuania, had died this way. He said he had grown up with her, played with her when young, and explored Palanga together. He said when they entered puberty, they started having sex, which seemed so normal, but this all changed when Ugne got pregnant. He said she was distraught and began talking about committing suicide, which alarmed him, so he stayed close to her and sometimes would hold her tight, hoping to make her feel better.

After a pause, Oscar said he had left her only briefly when she went to the barn and ate a handful of Dursban, a chlorpyrifos pesticide created by Dow Chemical in 1965 that's commonly used on corn, soybeans, broccoli, and apples, and it's widely used on golf courses. He said she ingested some poison in a moment of crisis. Many suicides happen impulsively like this, due to a breakdown in the ability to deal with life stresses, such as financial problems, relationship breakups, chronic pain, and illness. If poor Ugne had just waited an hour, she probably would not have done it. He said that when he returned, he saw her dizzy, sweating, and tearing, and immediately knew what she had done. He said he knew, like most insecticides, Drusban was killing enzymes that were essential for the normal operation of her nervous system. He said he again held young Ugne tightly as she began experiencing difficulty breathing, muscle tremors, abdominal cramps, and vomiting. Shaking uncontrollably, she started gasping for breath as her skin turned grey, her eyes rolled and froze, and her body gradually relaxed as she died in his arms. Tearful Oscar then said he loved Ugne and abruptly stopped talking because he was so distraught.

Fortunately, Iaso said, to avoid such painful deaths, some enlightened civilizations, like the State of Oregon in America, have passed laws legalizing suicide. Oregon's Death with Dignity Act allows a terminally ill Oregonian to end their life through voluntary self-administration of a lethal dose of medication prescribed by a physician. They must be eighteen or older, a resident of Oregon, capable of making and communicating health care decisions, and have been diagnosed with a terminal illness that will lead to death within six months, and the drug must be self-administered. The doctor usually prescribes a high quantity of fast-acting barbiturates—sedatives, usually pentobarbital and secobarbital—that puts them to sleep and quietly stops their bodily functions.

Even though it had been years since Ugne's death, Oscar said he still felt her loss, and along with the foreboding of his damaged heart, he had decided to join her. He said he went to the pharmacy and told the druggist he was having trouble sleeping and wanted to know what were some effective sedatives. The unwitting druggist suggested Aleve PM, Unisom Sleep Tabs, melatonin, or valerian. Oscar said he bought six bottles of the sleep-inducing barbiturate Aleve PM, went home, and swallowed them all. He said he quickly fell asleep and almost died. Unlike the pain and awareness of dying from a heart attack, he just fell asleep assuming he would never wake, but he did not take enough sedative to kill him.

Oscar said that when he eventually woke, after a really good night's sleep in a semi-comatose state, he was hit with an epiphany: how easy it is to die and hard to live. It is easier to exit life than stay in the game; living takes tremendous effort and courage. He said he began thinking about living and the joys he would miss if he had died. He realized he would miss his loving wife Madeline and his children, a good meal, a restful night's sleep, his lively friends, the joy of learning, the sights and smells of a beautiful fall day, and even the basketball games he usually lost. He said he asked himself why voluntarily leave early? And his answer was, Better to stay and enjoy whatever life was left for him to experience.

Smiling, wise Athena said, This is why exploring death explains what it means to live. Accepting death and deciding to live life, as Oscar did, enabled him to live a fuller life.

Philosophers on Suicide

Then the philosopher goddess Rhea told Oscar about some philosophers and their views on suicide, many of which were discussed earlier comparing the blessings and curses of death. She said that some philosophers, like Albert Camus, wrote, *There is only one philosophical problem which is really serious; suicide. To decide whether life is or is not worth living.* Along these lines, she said, a central tenet of the ancient school of Stoicism was the legitimacy of suicide. They, for example, advised suicide as a solution for unhappiness. Indeed, famous Stoic philosopher Seneca once wrote that *freedom is always near—just kill yourself.* She said, Anna Akhmatova wrote to Death in "Requiem," *You will come in any case—so why not now?*

But then Rhea asked Oscar, If death is the rule and living the exception, why not choose to live? Living is interesting, so why not enjoy the unusual experience?

Oscar thought for a bit and said that he supposed it depended on how good one's life was and the circumstances. Sure, he said, suicide was probably the right decision for my aged father facing a terminal disease, but what about a young person like Ugne who was healthy and young?

On a deeper level, there is an existential question about one's right to choose life or death, Rhea continued, regardless of circumstances. To decide not to live seems a natural right. Some people just don't like living, so why deny them an exit? It is almost cruel to make one live a life that keeps them in misery. Certainly, Ugne's death was tragic because it truncated so much potential future love, life, and happiness, unlike Oscar's ninety-year-old father Jonas Uzgalis, who had lived a full life, was dying from congestive heart disease, and committed legal suicide. There does exist a right to kill oneself, but it should be done thoughtfully, slowly, and with care.

The Ways Humans Die

Most ways humans die have been around for eons, but one new one is HIV, or human immunodeficiency virus, which attacks the immune system and can lead to AIDS, or acquired immune deficiency syndrome, if left untreated. AIDS is the term used to describe the severe damage done by the virus to the immune system. It destroys the system that prevents infections, so AIDS is death by infection. Certainly, dying from infection is an old way to die, but AIDS brought a new twist to the process by suppressing the body's immune system and its ability to fight infection.

HIV is one of the world's most infectious diseases. About one million people die each year from AIDS resulting from HIV, mostly in southern African countries. Most people get HIV through anal or vaginal sex, or by sharing needles, syringes, or other drug injection equipment.

Dying from AIDS-caused infection is a long-term and gruesome way to go. It usually begins with a nonhealing open sore, dry cough, tightness in the chest, coughing, fever, and shortness of breath. The lungs get a white haze, and the tongue gets coated with the telltale milky fungus of thrush. The victim becomes anemic, with fewer white blood cells causing malnourishment, severe headaches, nausea, confusion, sometimes meningitis, and lethargy. Infections occur everywhere, including the ear, armpit, and sinuses. The vulnerable lungs are the most common organ assaulted by the HIV virus, which causes pneumonia, leaving the victim gasping for oxygen, and ultimately death.

It was then that Euphrosyne, the goddess of good cheer, said excitedly that jolly Grimy was here just as the fun maker himself appeared. Grimy said he had heard that Oscar had a second heart attack, so he was here to see if he should be harvested. He said he wanted to make it quick because he had to leave Dionysus's party where he had been making good time with Aphrodite. He quickly asked Oscar if he was still in Limbo, and Oscar responded sarcastically that Grimy should know because it was him, along with Hades and Chaos, who had put him in that godforsaken never-never land. Unperturbed, Grimy said that fifty years ago, Oscar would have died, but modern medicine has saved him again, so Grimy will not be harvesting him now. With that he returned to Dionysus's party to try and bed Aphrodite.

CHAPTER 8
Traditional and Modern Death

THANATOS TOOK OVER THE DISCUSSION AND SAID, We will have to leave Oscar in Limbo a while longer because Grimy did not harvest him. He then told Oscar he should be giving more thought to his health and inevitable death due to his heart attacks.

He said, How you will die and how others deal with your death has changed dramatically in many societies. Indeed, there is more to death than just dying. Will your death be a good or bad one? Will it be comfortable or anxious? Will you die alone? Your attitude toward death and how you treat others will determine the answers to these questions.

Death today in many advanced societies is unnatural. It is no longer the old friend coming to ease your pain and take you somewhere, but rather an enemy to be feared and avoided. Dying used to be a rich, personal, meaningful, and intimate experience, and is now a cold, institutional, and solitary ending. Modern dying is very different from the way it used to be.

Traditional Death

It was then that the Gaia, goddess of earth, and Chronos, god of time, both said they remembered traditional death. Gaia said that humans know a lot about the old and new ways of dying, mostly from thanatologist David Wendell Moller, who had many insights, and from their *Encyclopedia of Death and Dying*, which is full of information on how humans die.

Death used to be a community affair. Take for example the death of Ramunas the farmer. Mehal was a simple man who lived in the country and spent his life working the family farm like his father and grandfather. One fateful day while he was plowing the back acreage, the plow got stuck, so he climbed off and reached into the blades to free them from some roots. Suddenly the idling tractor accidently kicked into gear and slowly dragged the sharp plow blades over Mehal's body, severing one arm, detaching a foot, severely lacerating his body, and piercing his abdomen. Mortally wounded, Mehal started bleeding profusely. He stumbled home, where his alarmed wife bandaged him as best she could. She called the doctor, family, and friends and told them Mehal had an acci-dent and may be dying.

As people flooded in, the doctor told Mehal his body was too mangled to repair and that he would die shortly, probably from shock due to the lack of blood. His friends exchanged intimate goodbyes with Mehal, his sister and brothers hugged him and said how much they loved him and will miss him, and his wife and four children climbed into his bloodstained bed to hold him in one warm and tender final embrace. There was kissing and tears and grief as Mehal gradually lost consciousness and died in their arms.

Even though Mehal was in terrible pain, he felt joy having said goodbye to all the people he loved, he felt good giving away his possessions, and he was satisfied when he gave his interest in the farm to his wife, children, and siblings. For Mehal it was his last joyful experience of life just before the last ounce of blood left his body. He went into convulsions from shock and died. Mehal had lived a good life and died in his bed at home surrounded by family and friends. He was happy and had no regrets. Mehal had a good traditional death.

Traditionally death was simple. Family, friends, and the entire community cared for the dying person. It was a public, conspicuous, and visible event, and someone was always dying. Death was the natural end of living, and everyone knew someone who was at the end of their life. Because of this, people were constantly reminded that they too would die, which took much of the fear out of the event. Their fatalistic view was that we are all in it together—life is short, and we all die. With this knowledge people took death in stride and were more resigned and accepting of its occurrence.

The reminders of mortality were everywhere. In literature, paintings, and cemeteries, people were constantly reminded of the specter of their death, which made it more acceptable. Religion in particular wove death into the fabric of life with rituals and ceremonies. The famous book *Ars moriendi*, which characterized the patterns of death with openness and acceptance, was known by heart to ardent Catholics.

It was then Momus, god of satire, writers, and poets, said he could attest that humans had written much on death, most of which is intense, serious doggerel.

Ars moriendi, which means "the art of dying" in Latin, was popular in the 1300 and 1400's during the Black Death, the most fatal pandemic in human history, in which 75 to 200 million people died. The book offered consolatory advice during unprecedented public death. It extolled Christian advice and protocols and procedures on how to die well. Some of its comforting lessons were:

dying has a good side and it should not be feared; the need to avoid common temptations of a dying person, such as lack of faith, despair, impatience, and avarice; the need to forgive ones' enemies and to restore ill-gotten goods; how friends and family should behave around a deathbed; and, poignantly, that everyone should prepare for their own inevitable deaths.

Unfortunately, continued Gaia, support for the dying does not come from books like *Ars moriendi* but rather people, especially family and friends. At your death you need comfort and support, which is given through loved ones, from the broader community as it mourns the loss of one of its members, and from the many the rituals, ceremonies, and prayers of religion. These lessons of traditional death have been largely lost to modern death, or dying with the experts.

Modern Death

Today death is a lonely, solitary affair. Take for example Ramunas's grandson Lukas, who eschewed his grandfather's simple way of life for a more exciting one in the city. Unlike his ancestors, Lukas went to the university and after graduation became a stockbroker. He made a lot of money, lived in a million-dollar downtown condominium, drove an expensive car, and rarely talked to his relations back home. He did not marry and lived alone, preferring freedom.

He was content until one day, while crossing a busy downtown street, he was hit by a car. It severed his lower spine and immediately paralyzed him from the waist down. Groaning, he was taken to the nearest hospital and rushed into the sterile, brightly lit emergency room where doctors and nurses went to work trying to keep him alive. After hours of work, the leading physician told him they had not been successful and that he would most likely die soon from septicemia.

Septicemia, or sepsis, is blood poisoning by bacteria. It is the body's most extreme response to an infection, and 50 percent of its victims die if it advances to septic shock. It occurs when chemicals are released in the bloodstream to fight infection trigger inflammation throughout the body.

Barely able to breathe, Lukas lingered for a few days in a small hospital room. He suffered fevers, low blood pressure, a racing heart, and mental confusion. Unlike his grandfather, he was alone in the room with strangers who cared little for him personally coming and going. There was no wife, children, or siblings, there was nobody to say intimate goodbyes to, and there was no kissing, embracing, or tears. He was alone with his pain, slowly dying under the sheets.

Finally, a cascade of physiologic changes due to sepsis engulfed his heart, lungs, blood vessels, kidneys, and liver, along with a drastic drop in blood pressure to shock levels that killed him. Lukas died alone. His death was not a joyful experience like his grandfather's, but rather a lonely dispirited one. Also, unlike his father and grandfather, Lukas died with regrets. His most powerful regret was not to marry and have a family, an unfulfilled potential. He always thought he had enough time to find the right woman and start a family, but time had run out. Lukas died a modern, lonely death among stranger experts.

Unlike rich, comforting, and meaningful traditional death, dying today has become sterile and lonely, much like Oscar's hospital stays after his first two heart attacks. Lukas found himself alone in a small, colorless hospital room with stark bright lights. Dying and grieving have become isolated, feared, ugly, and dirty events. Once a meaningful and integral part of social life, it has become a source of terror where the dying are vanquished from public visibility. Some describe this new way to die as a kind of a death taboo.

Oscar asked Gaia, Why is this? Why has the way we die changed to this?

Gaia said, Western society has redefined how you die for four reasons according to your David Moller: due to the advances of individualism, secularism, materialism, and science in society. With individualism the community has withdrawn from the dying process; unlike religion, secularism offers no meaning or comfort for the dying; materialism is ill-equipped to grapple with the mystery of death; and science, and its child technology, has enabled humanity to actively fight and delay death. This has made death no longer a natural, necessary, and significant part of life; rather, it has become the enemy that needs to be defeated. This denial of death has separated the dying from any cultural support and tragically brought about meaningless isolation and shame for the dying. It has put a stigma on death and caused an uncomfortable coverup.

The Stigma of Death

After listening to Gaia, Oscar exclaimed that he had experienced the societal stigma of dying firsthand. He said he had felt embarrassed dying, that he wanted to hide, and that he did not want his corpse to make a mess. He said he was ashamed of his disgusting, feeble dying body and the grief it would cause others, so he wanted his loved ones to stay away—he ardently wanted to die alone.

Gaia said, Competitive Western cultures that have embraced the new way of dying do not make people—and in particular, dying persons—feel good about themselves. These new cultures deem death so disgraceful that many of the dying are now quietly shuttled off to hideaway homes called hospice to die alone. She then said, These Western secular cultures vilify those who do not comport with societies idea of a good death and seriously stigmatize those marginalized sects who die from HIV/AIDS, substance abuse, and insanity, as well as those who die irregular deaths, including suicide and homicide.

Your thanatologist David Wendell Moller has documented individual humans' feelings about dying in this new stigmatized way. Comments from some of them reveal their profound suffering and thoughts about their own mortality and new isolated way of dying. Ones asks why God has deserted them. Another says their illness makes them want to withdraw from society and be alone (rather than seek its comfort). Most think they are not themselves anymore, they are not what they used to be, which makes them feel estranged from their own essence as a human. Many of those dying from cancer have no hope because there is nothing positive happening in their life. For all of them, it is a physically and emotionally confusing and depressing process that makes them want to commit suicide, which some do.

The Uncomfortable Coverup

Chronos then took over from Gaia and said, The modern way to die has brought about a strange new silent coverup where everyone knows a person is dying but they do not talk about it or acknowledge it. There are many reasons for this, including the modern stigma of dying, fear of hurting the feelings of the one dying, and the inconveniences death causes to the living. It is a strange phenomenon indeed when everyone knows someone dying, but they ignore it.

It is particularly hard on the one dying, because they know everyone knows they are dying but don't talk about it, so the one dying also does not talk about it. This makes the dying person feel isolated and lonely because they want to talk with others about what is happening to them, but they are afraid to break the silence. The silence, evasion, and pretense surrounding death today is like the one-thousand-pound elephant in the room that nobody admits exists. To make matters worse for the dying, everyone is in on the coverup. Family members and fellow workers remain strangely silent as well as the medical experts who are treating the dying person.

It was here that Oscar became quite excited and described his hospital experience after his heart attacks. He said, It is subtle but real. When the medical staff thought I was going to die, despite their good intentions, they started separating themselves from me, and the depersonalization began. It was like they gradually stopped treating me as a human being because I was going to be corpse shortly. In a strangely paternal way, it was like my parents tucking me in bed for the night, but this time it was the nurses who were preparing me for the morgue. I felt surrounded by bad actors playing their part in a horror B-movie about my death. There was nobody to have a real, honest conversation and last words with.Having that would be a rarity in intensive care units.

Oscar continued, It was a strange and lonely experience that only got worse when I recovered. I went back to work at my government job, but because my coworkers thought I could die any moment from a heart attack, nobody wanted to talk about my experience. It was like a conspiracy where everyone pretended I had no problems and everything was normal, while inside I was yearning to talk about my feelings, the dying experience, and the afterlife. This living on an empty stage made me feel alone, helpless, and worthless when what I really needed was human contact, care, and understanding.

The Identity Dilemma

Thanatos began talking, but he was quickly interrupted by Koalemos, the god of stupidity and ignorance. Koalemos, who always has a chip on his shoulder, told Thanatos he was a pomp-ous ass, to which Thanatos said, Only a stupid god could be the god of stupidity.

It was then that a thunderbolt flashed, striking fear in everyone. Zeus appeared, the god of gods, who said, Get along or I will strip you of your godhood.

Koalemos said that he thought he was best to describe humans' identity dilemma because it derives from ignorance. He said, Earlier, another human dilemma was described: whether humans are in or out of nature. It was said that due to humans' unique mind, they have transcended nature, but because their mind is trapped in a body that rots, they are at the same time hopelessly in nature. Similar to this dilemma is the question of whether humans are naturally collective or individual. Humans spend their lives in collective society, but when they die, they die alone as an individ-ual. Nobody can die another's death.

This latter dilemma was not a problem during the traditional way to die because humans died with each other. But with the advent of modern death, they leave that collective society and die alone, usually in a sterile hospital or hospice room. For many reasons this new individualistic perspective is a source of terror for those who have spent their lives being a member of collective society. They fear losing social identity, having no social situation, not belonging to society, losing social relations, and social isola-tion. They particularly fear the modern way to die—alone among strangers. It is a dilemma for them because, on one hand, they want to be part of something, but on the other, they want to be free individuals. The change in the way they die has exacerbated this inherent contradiction.

It is interesting to observe how some unique humans handle this dilemma. Creative people, in particular artists, solve this problem by creating their own meaning outside of societies created meanings. Some of them thrive, some experience tremendous guilt, and a few become mad. Indeed, madness has always been humans' last sanctuary.

My opinion is that this is a false dichotomy, a dilemma manufactured by ignorant people who ardently wish to preserve the traditional, collective way of life and death. The truth is people die alone. Indeed, death itself is the deepest kind of solitude, divorced from collective society. Those dying are leaving on their final journey by themselves.

The Consequences of the Modern Way to Die

Metis thanked Koalemos for his explanation and then turned to Oscar and said, He is right as far as he goes, but there have been some unfortunate unintended consequences of the modern way to die. One is the difference between what the dying person and others think.

What the Dying Person Thinks and What Others Think

Because dying has become a highly personal and individual process, the one dying naturally thinks their death is catastrophic and profound, whereas others think it is a mere inconvenience. The modern dying person thinks their death is the most important event in the world because they will be gone and the world will suffer because they are not present. They find it hard to figure who will do their job and take their responsibilities. Indeed, they would be surprised to discover someone is secretly happy to see them go.

Because individualism has created a zeitgeist where everyone is on their own, others think little of the person who is dying. The dying think everyone is thinking about them when in truth everyone is thinking about themselves. Earlier, the thoughts of

Oscar's family and friends were described while he was dying. One complained about having to go to his funeral, another to have to give up their nap, a few complained about having to send a condolence letter, one did not want to travel so far to his funeral, some greedy relatives wanted inheritance, and a coworker hoped to get his job and a promotion. The modern way of dying exacerbates these kinds of attitudes toward the dying. Other's deaths are simply no big deal.

Being Special

A second similar change is that the dying person thinks they are special. Individualism makes them think they are the center of society rather than part of it. This is a self-serving belief that the human philosopher Rochefoucauld revealed when he wrote how insignificant human life is; people think only about themselves and rarely others. Just consider that worldwide about 150,000 humans die every day, which is about 6,250 deaths per hour, 104 deaths per minute, and around two deaths every second. To die is not special.

Eternal Hope

Another human philosopher, Alexander Pope, once wrote, *Blessed is he who expects nothing, for he shall never be disappointed.* The modern way to die changes this because individuals believe they are special and entitled to a better life, and they expect to be honored after they die. They have excessive and unjustified hope for a better future and sometimes afterlife.

With this observation by Metis, Elpis, the god of hope, got into a heated argument with Algea, the gods of pain and suffering. Elpis denied that hope causes pain and suffering, to which visibly agitated Algea said, The opposite is true—it is hope that ameliorates pain and suffering.

Algea said, Just look at the unhappiness the loss of hope causes. It is hope that sustains people; it is an essential ingredient for a successful and happy life. Just consider the lyrics from the song "The Rose" that describes a heart afraid of breaking and afraid to walk that never lives.

Elpis retorted, You are wrong, just look at the unhappiness that is caused to those whose high hopes have been thwarted. Indeed, the ones with the greatest hopes are the most disappointed and sad when they die alone the modern way.

Cancerous Regret

Metis then said, One final unintended consequence of modern death is excessive and unwarranted regret. It has been said that regret is the cancer of life, and dying with regret can be as painful as dying from cancer. Compare, for example, how the traditional and modern ways to die play out in some common regrets dying people experience. Some of these include unresolved conflicts, breached relationships, unfulfilled potential, promises not kept, and years never to be lived.

Unresolved conflicts intensify because people had fewer of them when they considered themselves part of the whole, or an integral part of society. The same is true of breached relationships, because those who lived and died traditional deaths had fewer conflicts and thus failed relationships. Put another way, self-regarding people breach relationships, whereas other-regarding people maintain them. Imagine the unhappiness caused by a dying person who is angry at the unfulfilled potential of their life. This is exacerbated by modern death because the individual is thinking only of them-selves, whereas under traditional death the individuals' highest potential was often achieved within the group.

Promises not kept is another regret of those dying that the modern way to die intensifies because there is less personal responsibility to others, unlike the collective traditional ways of life and death. Finally, the regret over the years that will never be lived is made intolerable by the modern way to die because those dying think they are special whereas, as discussed earlier, collectivism tells them they are not, that they have lived long enough, and that they will die and soon be forgotten, just like everyone else.

Dying the traditional way did not emphasize these sources of regret because they were dampened by the weight of society. Dying the modern, lonely, individual way reinforces and justifies these regrets because the individual thinks everything that happens only happens to them, which engenders anger, resentment, and more regret.

The Ways Humans Die

It was then that Hygeia, who has described many of the ways humans die, said, About the worst way they die is from cancer, because it involves suffering pain for a long time. Cancer is the Latin word for *crab* because cancer's tentacles look like a crab. It is a disease of altered maturation—the unrestrained growth of cells, called *tumors* or *malignant neoplasms*. These tumors obstruct organs, inhibit metabolic processes, erode blood vessels and cause bleeding, and destroy vital body centers, usually the bones and liver. Early on its symptoms are poor nutrition, debilitation, susceptibility to infection, weakness, and the gradual wasting of muscles and other tissues. As the disease progresses, cancer cells force their way into nearby structures and prevent them from functioning. The final stage of cancer involves abscesses, urinary infections, a gradual decrease in blood pressure, and unremitting pain. Cancer causes death by restricting the flow of oxygen and nutrients to the body, which ultimately leads to sepsis and shock, causing the liver or kidneys to fail.

The survival rate from cancer depends on the type of cancer. Melanoma and prostate cancer, for example, have very high survival rates, whereas pancreatic cancer is almost always fatal. On average, 40 percent of cancer patients survive after five years from diagnosis, a milestone that greatly reduces their odds of it recurring.

Oscar then said to Hygeia that he had known a young Irish woman named Aoife, pronounced *Ee-fa*, who had died from ovarian cancer. He said, She was a wonderful, happy woman enjoying life with her husband and three children. Her name in Irish means *beautiful, joyful, and radiant,* which she was. One day out of nowhere, she started having pelvic and abdominal pain, nausea, and indigestion. She went to her doctor, who asked what other symptoms she was experiencing, and, worried, she said frequent urination, lack of energy, and constipation. The doctor told her these were classic symptoms of ovarian cancer, and after some tests, that she had it. She might live another year, he said, and she would most likely die when the cancer invaded her bone marrow.

Aoife was devastated, but she soldiered on, doing her best to care for her family. Gradually, the pain was so intense she became bedridden. She did her best to not complain about the terrible pain, but you could see it in her eyes.

Algea said, You cannot imagine the agony poor Aoife was enduring. Just listen to some of her private thoughts during her last few days alive (these are the actual words, taken from David Moller's website, of a woman who was dying from cancer):

> Oh God the pain is so great. To sleep and feel normal, then to awake with such pain! I want to die. I can't live with this newness. There are so many tubes in my

body. Every orifice. My hair is gone, my head is a giant bandage. Why can't I just die? I retreat to a resignation that most things in life are empty-colorless-undesirable. Because of all this, most days I try not to look in the mirror, so I can still pretend that I look like anything other than a cancer patient. It seems that everything keeps going back to this cancer. It makes me feel so ugly, and it's just so depressing. I can't even stand to look in the mirror anymore

With that, as her distraught young family watched, tears begin to stream from frail Aoife's eyes. Her silent thoughts continued:

I'm no good to anybody. Why am I living? Why doesn't God just let me die? I feel so useless, and I'm a burden to everyone. This is no way to live. The pain, oh why? I'm just no good. Everything seems to lead me back to my cancer. Cancer, cancer, that's it! That's all there is. I'm just wasting my life away. Having cancer is so time consuming. It doesn't make me feel well, feel good or happy. It's boring and painful. There's nothing positive! All it does is hurt. Everybody!

Aoife's last thoughts before she died that are the most tragic. She thought:

I cannot stand this, my husband can barely look at me, he finds my frail cancer-ridden body repulsive, and my appearance terrifies my children. I feel awful looking this way and leaving my husband and young children. What will my husband do when I am gone? Will he remarry? How will my children grow up without me? Who will love and mother them when I am gone? But there is nothing I can do. I just want to die and be gone.

Hygeia then said to Oscar, This is the voice of agony and regret of the dying. Aoife's thoughts reflect the isolation and terror modern death magnifies. Her regret is a common one —the years never to be lived. In this case, her death is harmful because it is taking from a young person future happiness—in Aoife's case, happy events with her family while watching her children grow up. To make matters worse, under the modern way to die, Aoife is dying in a state of exile and enduring her suffering in isolation. Indeed, she keeps her sad thoughts to herself as the experts watch her suffer in silence.

Thanatos thanked Hygeia and Oscar for their descriptions of cancer. He said he had been so affected by Aoife's suffering that he had immediately sent her on her final journey. He then turned to Oscar and said, I am sorry to tell you, but you have to stay in Limbo a while longer because Grimy did not harvest you after your second heart attack. Let us now move on and describe the ways humans deal with their fear of death.

CHAPTER 9

Strategies for Avoiding the Fear of Death

Thanatos looked at Oscar and said, Because you have made death your enemy, the thought of it has robbed you of the meaning of life and has put you in solitary confinement. It is no surprise, then, that you feel alone in the universe. Earlier death was described as your peculiar and quietest anxiety that pits your ethereal mind against your physical body, which causes you to create strategies to overcome it. Because these strategies originate in your fear of death, I have asked Phobos to describe some of them.

The Fear of Death

Phobos, the ironic embodiment of cowardliness and fear, told Oscar, Humans are a strange species, because it seems every time they start contemplating eternal problems like death, they become fearful and anxious, which narrows their mind to small problems. This usually results in a refusal to acknowledge reality. It is a kind of grand state of denial imbued with a deep existential panic.

You, for example, work hard to keep your mind from thinking about death, which is very common. You work all the time but eventually get burned out, as you say, so you take a vacation thinking it will bring peace of mind. But when you take two weeks off, your mind is left free to think, and thinking often turns to thoughts of death, which causes you tremendous angst. So you cut your vacation short and go back to work in order to escape your fear of death thoughts, only to get burned out again. But returning to work only restarts your cycle of fear of death-work-burnout-vacation-fear of death-work. It is a vicious circle where excessive work burns you out and the ostensible solution, a vacation, only makes matters worse.

Many of your strategies are narrow, like work and a vacation, and others profound. Let me describe some of them in more detail.

Strategies

Some of your trivial strategies, or myths, to avoid thinking about death make you look like a trembling animal who pulls the world down around themselves in its attempt to forget its grotesque fate. For example, Oscar, you often tell yourself, Just don't think about it. You endeavor to forget about dying and rotting. Another of your shallow ways includes denying that it happens at all. You often, for example, think that the person next to you will die someday but not you. I am sorry, but these strategies don't work. You cannot ignore what you already know is true. It is like standing on a freeway thinking you are immaterial and getting run over by a bus.

Following are a few more of your more sophisticated strategies. The first is religion, which has been with you for thousands of years.

The Failure of Religion

Superstition, religion, and faith have historically been your main defense against thinking about that impenetrable black void. Your shamans have conceived of some very imaginative and sometimes fantastic nostrums to balm your fear of death, some of which have been described.

Their creativeness impresses me. Those in your primitive, superstitious societies were most imaginative when dealing with death. Your priests conceived numerous fairytales, some of which make you immortal, some of which conceive of places you go when you leave this world, and some of which made you ignorant. They claimed only they could divine God's plan. Religion's two myths that have given you the most comfort are heaven and reincarnation. You have found these myths appealing, especially the idea of heaven.

Your religions have always preached the haven of Heaven. In ancient Mesopotamia heaven was called Dir-an-ki; in Greece Empyrean fields; under Christianity the Kingdom of Heaven, which is the throne of God; and in Confucianism Tian. Some of your ancient religions, like Buddhism, Islam, and Aztec beliefs, even postulated numerous heavens.

The idea of being reborn through reincarnation is another of your prophets' imaginative ideas that makes you happy because you never die. But this strategy, more than any other, unveils your prophets' agenda, which is to get you to follow them. Reincarnation, for example, is a central tenant in Hinduism, and the Hindu priests always imagine you returning as a fat, happy sacred cow that freely wanders the streets of Bombay eating the handouts from believers. They rarely have you come back as a lowly sardine that gets eaten by a seagull.

Your religion is uniquely suited to shield you from your fear of death. Having faith in an afterlife, for example, makes you humans happy. It gives you hope in this existentialist nonteleological void of existence. It also gives answers to fundamental questions that disciplines like psychology and biology don't. Those disciplines do not ask who humans are, why they are here, and why they die. Religion does not surrender to nature and seek a higher meaning for you—it makes you more than meat. Also, because religion, and the gods it proposes, are so wonderfully abstract, virtually any scheme can be custom written to balm anyone's' fears of death. In this way your religion and its gods are perfect.

But there are downsides to this religious, insular way of thinking. First, everyone down deep knows that religions' preaching is not necessarily true. Indeed, they are probably wrong. Second, its preaching is only as good as the strength of its followers' faith, and if their faith fails, so does the religious belief. Finally, as your famous philosopher Spinoza pointed out, many of the attributes you give to your religious lawgiver gods are obviously attributes that are in your interests for them to have. Wishing, for example, that your god would be omnibenevolent, protecting you from death, reveals your selfish reason for worshipping it with that attribute—such as the fear of death.

Phobos then said, One other important but academically stultifying consequence of religion's effort to balm the fear of death is predestination. Humans like to think they have free will, independent judgment and choice, but they labor under the great religious claim that everything is determined.

With that, a quarrel broke out among some gods. Nemesis, goddess of retribution and vengeance, told Phobos he was an easily spooked coward, especially when he looked in the mirror. She said that his fear of the Fates was well known because they were the only entity that overrode the gods. She accused Phobos of taking sadistic delight in tormenting humans with fear. She said, Of course all is determined—including your own death, Phobos—and that all human strategies, including free will, to avoid it are doomed.

Then Chronos, the confused old god of time, told Nemesis that her vengeful anger was a waste of time and that time was running out.

Red-faced Phobos, who was obviously angry at Nemesis, and determined Chronos were about to get into a tempestuous godly fight, which often sends out hurricanes to the humans. Kratos, the god of strength and power, forcefully told them all to cool it. He told Nemesis to leave Phobos alone, told Cronos to go back to sleep, and urged Phobos to continue his story.

Phobos regained his composure and said certainly, The religious Fates take all questions about death out of our hands. The Moirai, or Fates in English, are three weaving older goddesses of destiny. Clotho is the spinner who spins humans' life destinies; Lachesis is the allotter who draws their destinies out; and Atropos is the unturnable—a metaphor for death—one who cuts the thread of life. The Fates are manifestations of religious predestination, and their role is to ensure that every being lives out the destiny, described as a thread spun from a spindle, that was assigned them.

Sure, religion brought humans hope of an afterlife that made them feel better, but the irony of all this is that religion, which they invented as a strategy to avoid the fear of death, ended up being deterministic. Many of their strategies fail because all is determined. So religion as a comfort has naturally faded from human history because it claimed to know things it did not, and the faith it required to maintain its illusions gradually failed in the face of reality. So religion and its theology naturally disappeared like a puff of smoke in a strong breeze.

Tyche, the goddess of fortune and prosperity, and Chaos, the god of nothingness, will discuss determinism and materialism in more detail shortly.

Pleasure and Chemicals

There are numerous other rather pedestrian ways humans have tried to avoid thinking about death. Indulging in pleasure, whether it be sex, food, or drugs, has been a favorite for millennia.

These could be described as a kind of human Epicurean descent into their animal natures in order to avoid thinking about what they know is true. When they stop thinking about controlling their base natures, their inner thoughts disappear and their body takes over, which allows them to wallow in unthinking pleasure. Unfortunately, the pleasure strategy fails because their desire is insatiable—they are never completely satisfied and are always left wanting more. The same is true of their use of chemicals as a strategy. Throughout history humans have used a variety of drugs to make them forget their fate. They have used tobacco, cannabis, cocaine, heroin, methamphetamine, alcohol, speed, peyote, and mescaline along with a long list of alcoholic drinks like cacao wine, Ninkasi beer, Egyptian herbal wine, barley beer, chicha, Hajji Firuz Tepe wine, mead, and a Chinese fermented beverage from as early as 5000 BCE, to forget. But, as with sex, the effects wear off quickly.

Prestige, Power, and Work

Three other common strategies for forgetting about death include prestige, power, and work. Pursuing titles and honors distracts them, and pursuing power makes them feel invincible, as if they are in total control of their life and death. Many immerse themselves in work in order to avoid thinking about the inevitable. They think it makes them a better provider, a better citizen, and a valuable asset to society, which makes them feel important. But this strategy also fails because when they are not working, they quickly relapse into their old fearful thoughts of death. All these strategies fail because they are just temporary patches that do not endure. In the end their fear of death always returns.

Empty Isolation

In some respects, the fear of death is a human herd fear. The fear is magnified because others fear of it also. Hushed voices talking about who has some fatal disease, whispers about who is dying, and anxious comments about who has died, along with furtive glances, reveal an underground world of peoples' deepest fear.

To avoid this inflaming source of fear, some, like Henry David Thoreau, have sought solitude. While living alone on Walden Pond, Thoreau's fear of death was not inflamed by others. It may well be that your Rousseau was right in a way: society does corrupt, but unfortunately this strategy does not eliminate the fear of death; it only mitigates it.

Other Strategies for Avoiding the Fear of Death

Unlike the previous failed strategies, the next two, illusion and mental illness, are spontaneously natural. It was here that Mania, goddess of insanity, said, There are many reasons that humans create illusions and go mad, but the fear of death is certainly one of them. For most humans death is their enemy, which leads to self-deception, robs them of meaning in life, and sends them to solitary confinement. For many humans, trying to deny their grotesque fate is the source of their illusions and madness. It is hard for them to appear sane when riven by their fear of death.

Illusion

Many humans escape into illusion to avoid the fear of death and thus remain happy and well-adjusted. They use illusion because they cannot live with the truism that they will die. Indeed, the very mental health of individuals depends on the strength of their illusions, or myths, or neuroses, because, as your psychologist Otto Rank pointed out, without illusions they would go mad. As odd as it may sound, humans cannot live with the truth of death. They must have salubrious illusions, like dignity and hope, to balm their pain of living and dying.

Perhaps the best example of this comes from your infamous Harvard professor and LSD user Timothy Leary, who always trying to get to the other side, without success. For him, becoming dead was just the first step in moving beyond life into a new beginning, or the other side. Unfortunately, brain-addled Leary could only describe the other side in metaphors because he had no true information on the other side—nobody ever reported back. It may well be that Leary's other side is nothingness, but it was the illusion that kept him happily sane. Ironically, those with the strongest illusions, like Leary, are sometimes called normal and those with no illusions are called neurotic.

The problem with illusions, however, is that because they are in constant conflict with reality, they eventually break down. Leary's other side failed because he could never get there, even with LSD. So when the illusions people imagine to avoid the fear of death fail, the result is usually psychotic mental illness.

Mental Illness

When their illusions fail, many humans go mad. Many think mental illness is due to one's genes, the environment, or a chemical imbalance, which is true in some cases. But madness is mostly a strategy to avoid the fear of death.

Those who have lost their illusions have trouble living with the truth of their existence, which includes their death, so they narrow the world, shut off experience, and fashion their own psychotic defenses. Deeply religious people, for example, who suddenly lose their faith are thrown lost, sad, confused, and anxious into an existential uncaring world. So they retreat into their last line of defense, which is their mind. In it they fashion an alternate reality to make themselves feel better. Because their alternate reality does not match reality, others think them strange when they merrily talk to themselves. It is a refuge that involves glib and empty talk to reinforce their alternate reality and mitigate the terror they carry in their hearts about their death. They try to cover their psychosis and pass themselves off as normal.

These poor souls exist in a living hell, fearful their ruse will be discovered, fearful they will not be able to maintain their alternate reality, and fearful of dying. With their effort to avoid misery, their descent into mental illness remains tenuous, and those that lose it often become catatonic or commit suicide.

So, Mania concluded, none of these ways to avoid the fear of death succeed. Faith in religion, the empty pursuit of sensual pleasure, false self-imposed illusion, and wayward detached mental illness all fail.

With that, Elpis, the goddess of hope, said, Let me offer some alternate practical ways—some inward and others outward—for humans to gain some felicity with knowing their fate.

The always peevish Nemesis was heard cynically whispering, Now we get to hear from the confused Don Quixote of the metaphysical world.

Practical Ways for Avoiding the Fear of Death

After giving Nemesis the evil eye, Elpis said, There are many other salubrious ways for humans to avoid thinking about their deaths and to live meaningful lives. The first comes from within.

The World Is as You Make It

The objective here is for humans to try to use their minds to stop thinking about and fearing death. They should be grateful for their experiences and live in the present, they should focus on making the most of their lives, they should be grateful for what they have, they should be creative because it makes them feel alive, and they should have a sense of purpose. Aristotle believed that there is purpose to existence. His famous example from nature is that the purpose of an acorn is to become an oak tree. Having a sense of purpose in life helps humans overcome their fear of death because they are part of some larger plan.

The second way is to act outwardly, to do something that detracts humans from fearing their fate. They should talk with others about their fear of death, they should indulge in death humor, they should go back to school and learn something they always wanted to know, they should find a sport and work at getting better at it, they should travel, they should find some meaningful work or avocation, they should learn to play a musical instrument, they should read the best books ever written, they should write their autobiography, they should get a pet, and finally they should enhance their relationships with other people. With these activities humans become so immersed in everyday living they don't have time to think about dying.

Rhea told Elpis that his practical ways to avoid thinking about death were just distractions, short-term-stopgap solutions. She looked at Oscar and said, The best ways are to accept and practice death.

Accept Death

If humans, Rhea continued, accept the fact they will die someday, there would be no need for strategies to avoid thinking about it. Accepting your death, Oscar, has been a central theme in this discussion because death is a natural process, like being born. Many good things happen when you do so. First, you no longer fear death. It is better to live with hope than fear. Second, you no longer worry about the future. It was mentioned earlier that the loss of your futures through death caused unhappiness. Indeed, not having a future to plan for is unsettling, but when you accept death, these foreboding thoughts vanish because you have accepted the fact that you have no future and no need for plans. Finally, when you accept death, you focus on living and the result is a fuller and happier life. Many of your philosophers have emphasized this point. Your Cicero wrote, *The man without the fear of death has secured a valuable aid toward a happy life*, and Seneca: *It is not how long the play lasts, but how good it is*. Also, keep in mind the old proverb that you only die once.

Practice Death

But it is not enough to just accept death, Rhea continued, you must also practice it.

To get good at anything, you must practice it. Let me ask you, Oscar, do you think you could be a great basketball player without practice?

Intrigued, Oscar said that he used to work very hard at drills and strategies in basketball in order to improve his game.

Well, said Rhea, death is the same. You must anticipate and practice it in order to be good at it. This is a point that many of your philosophers have emphasized. Seneca wrote, *Rehearse death; it is a very good thing to familiarize oneself with death*, and Epictetus, *When you kiss your child, you should say to yourself tomorrow you may be dead.* Every morning you should remind yourself that this could be your last day alive, because it just might be.

Ways Humans Die

Asclepius, the god of health and medicine, thanked Rhea for her explanations and said to Oscar, Rhere are so many ways humans die, many described by us here, that it is amazing you humans live long at all. Looking at Oscar, he said he was particularly concerned about him because he had had two heart attacks, and he noticed that he was again showing some ominous symptoms. You faint frequently, fatigue easily, become winded when you exercise, often experience dizziness and lightheadedness, and have complained about heart palpitations or sudden, intense pounding in your chest. Most significantly, you have experienced fibrillation, or an irregular and often very rapid heart arrhythmia.. These are symptoms of heart disease and indicate you need a pacemaker.

Worried, Oscar went to his cardiologist shortly afterwards, who told him he needed a pacemaker. So they inserted an implantable cardiac defibrillator (ICD), or pacemaker, under Oscar's skin. It was implanted in his chest just below his collar bone with two wires connected to the chambers of his heart. The device sent small electrical currents to Oscar's heart if it beat too slowly, too fast, or stopped—in other words, it kept his heart beating regularly. Oscar's doctor told him that he would have to come back in about ten years to replace the battery. Oscar's life was now dependent on a battery.

With that Thanatos looked at Oscar and said, I must remind you again to look after your health, even with a pacemaker, or you will die soon. Like most humans, you have devised numerous strategies to avoid your fear of death, strategies that we have described, as well as many from your philosophers and literary figures. These are crutches you have used to escape your angst over dying, which have made you less concerned about your health. However, my colleagues have given you a number of reasons why they fail; accepting and practicing death are the only exceptions. Your central historical strategy has been religion, and some more sophisticated ones have been illusion and mental illness, but they all have failed.

Next, Rhea, the goddess of nature, and the wisest philosopher among us, will explain to you the ultimate reasons your strategies fail.

Oscar said, take your time, because I am not looking forward to Grimy's next visit. I am getting kind of used to this Limbo place.

CHAPTER 10

Why the Strategies for Avoiding the Fear of Death Fail

You may recall that this story about Oscar Uzgalis's death began with the gods on Mt. Olympus discussing why humans fear death. After a lively debate, Kratos, god of strength and power, and Ares, god of chaos and war, decided that it was because humans were confused and thus didn't understand the nature of death. This new discussion, soon to be donnybrook, was about whether humans' clever strategies for avoiding their fear of death worked.

The Gods Debate Human Strategies for Avoiding the Fear of Death

Tyche, goddess of fortune and prosperity, and Chaos, god of nothingness, were adamant that humans' strategies were successful because there was a world outside of materialism, free will existed, and humans had a subconscious. Put another way, they forcefully argued that there is a world humans can manipulate. The immaterial mind, or soul, is real and capable of determining humans' fate in ways that cannot always be understood. Because of this, humans can devise ways to avoid their dread of death.

Rhea, the goddess of nature and the wisest philosopher among the gods, strongly disagreed. She had already claimed that all of their strategies fail. She said, There is no world beyond perception, everything is determined, and all existence is material. This statement precipitated an intense, almost violent, debate between Tyche, Chaos, and Rhea.

Sensing that their argument could cause another tsunami or war killing thousands of humans, Thanatos interceded and said he was not sure who was right. Earlier, he had asked whether there was something metaphysical, like an observing soul or just the physical brain, watching through the senses. He said he suspected all was material.

It was then that Nyx, the shadowy goddess of night who rides in a chariot pulled by two dark horses, Shade and Shadow, told Thanatos to shut up.

Thanatos cowered and his face went pale. She was the only god he feared, because she was his mother. Nyx criticized Thanatos for being a noncommittal coward and said that Chaos was right, everything sprang from the void of nothingness, which means there could very well be another world.

This greatly irritated Rhea, who said they should ask Oscar, a human, what he thought, to which all agreed.

Oscar's Reflections on His Family and Materialism

Thanatos summoned a recalcitrant Oscar and reminded him of the excuses he had devised to avoid thinking about death and the many reasons his fellow gods had given why they all fail, especially religion.

By this time Oscar had lost all fear of the gods. He told them to leave him alone and to tell Grimy he was an asshole because Oscar was getting bored in Limbo. He said, I am tired of you officious, meddling gods interfering with my life. For me, he exclaimed, there is no free will because you damn gods keep determining what happens to me.

But if you really want to know if all is material, you should summon my ancestors Gabrielius and William Uzgalis and their descendants who, in a blood feud like the Hatfields and McCoys, have debated this issue for centuries. You may recall that Gabrielius was a Catholic bishop who believed in an afterlife and William was a philosophy professor inclined to materialistic and naturalistic explanations. Indeed, because my family's name means "beyond the end," they have a lot to say—too often about things of which they know nothing.

Thanatos then asked Charon, the ferryman of all dead souls, especially those from the Underworld, to bring Gabrielius and William to Mt. Olympus. When they arrived, they were befuddled because they did not know where they were or why. But as soon as they saw each other, they started bickering and tossing insults. Gabrielius told William he looked as anemically sick as the last time he saw him, and William told Gabrielius he still looked like the same gaunt, syphilis-ridden shell he was on his deathbed. Gabrielius said to William that his secularism made humans miserable.

William retorted, No, the opposite is true. It is you who make humans miserable with your silly superstitions, like Heaven and Hell. Indeed, William continued, in order to avoid the evil god dilemma, you are the one who invented the free will that so confounds humans.

Exasperated Rhea, backed up by Athena, said, This is an old issue that goes back to the famous human philosopher Plato and his forms, and more recently to Descartes, who postulated dualism, or a separate mind and body. If dualism is true, then there might be an afterlife for the mind independent of the body, but if dualism is not true, then an afterlife is impossible for an independent mind because it needs a body to exist. But we know through our senses that real things exist, we know we are made up of bones and muscles—which is materialism—and we know that any effort to postulate a soul, an unconscious, or a heaven is pure speculation. They do not exist, because everything is material, which means all human strategies to avoid the fear of death fail.

Athena said she agreed with Rhea, but there was more to the story. She said, Humans' ability to change their thinking also depends on their having free will, and if determinism is true, they cannot alter the flow of history, which, like materialism, means all of their strategies fail. If all is material and determined, then humans' lot is to die and rot, and there is nothing they can do about it.

Materialism

However, continued Athena, before we discuss determinism, Rhea, Elpis, and I will demonstrate materialism with three examples: Phineas Gage, Grey Walter's Carousel, and near-death experiences. With that, Gabrielius and William were excused.

Phineas Gage's Personality

Athena asked Charon to bring Dr. John Harlow to them because, as Phineas's physician, he knew the story better than anyone. The doctor was thrilled when he was introduced to the gods. He knew each of them by name and power and said he was honored to be asked about his most famous patient. He said, Phineas's case is important in medicine, and many other disciplines like psychology and philosophy, because it is the first time a case inexorably revealed the brain's role in determining personality.

Dr. Harlow said that Phineas had been a highly respected and competent foreman on a railroad crew. He was well-balanced and efficient, capable, smart, energetic, and persistent in executing his plans. Unfortunately, one day while he was directing some rock-blasting work, a charge went off prematurely and drove a six-foot iron tamping rod through his head, penetrating his brain's frontal lobe. When I first saw him, it was an ugly wound, with a huge metal rod that entered just below his chin and exited through the top of his head. Phineas was calm and conscious, but his wound looked so bad everyone expected him to die. A coffin and burial clothes were made ready. However, he recovered, but his personality changed.

Dr. Harlow then speculated that the accident had destroyed the equilibrium between Gage's intellectual faculties and animal propensities. He said, He became fitful, irreverent, indulged in profanity—which he never did before—and showed little dereference to others. He became impatient with restraints that conflicted with his desires, obstinate, capricious, and vacillating. He also devised future plans that were quickly abandoned, and he spoke little. He acted like an animal who blindly follows its passions. For those who had known Phineas before the accident, such as his family, friends and myself, he was no longer Phineas, but rather someone else.

After his accident his employers would not rehire him because of his changed personality, so he moved for a time to Chile and worked as a stage coach driver. Eventually he returned to America, suffered multiple epileptic seizures, and died in May of 1860.

Rhea then asked Dr. Harlow why this case was so medically significant. The doctor paused for a minute to gather his thoughts and then said, Because so much of his brain had been physically altered. If the rod had penetrated his rear cerebellum, he would have died instantly because it would have interfered with his breathing and circulation. But it had penetrated and destroyed a large part of his forward cerebrum, which did not kill him but changed his personality.

Rhea then asked the doctor whether this frontal lobe damage that changed Phineas's character was an example of the brain's critical role in determining who we are. Put another way, she said, knowing this case, do you think our personalities are governed by a material brain, hence all is material?

Dr. Harlow paused long, looked at Rhea, and said, That is a bold assertion that is probably true.

Grey Walter's Carousel

Athena said, There is another ingenious human experiment done by Dr. W. Grey Walter, a British neurosurgeon, who explored whether humans' decisions are materially based. Dr. Walter wanted to prove that bursts of recorded brain activity were the initiators of intentional actions. So Athena asked Charon to bring Dr. Walter so he could describe his experiment.

When the doctor arrived, he was curious about the gods and their interest in him but mostly wanted to talk with Asclepius, the god of health and medicine. He asked Asclepius if humans would ever discover a cure for Alzheimer's. Asclepius said that he could tell the doctor much about health and medicine but he could not foretell the future. He said that he was just as interested as the doctor as to whether humans would find a cure for the disease. He said that humans had been most ingenious curing past illnesses and hoped they could find a cure for this one.

Athena then asked Dr. Walter to describe his unusual experiment. Honored to be asked, the doctor said that he wanted to know what caused human actions, so he devised this carousel experiment. He said, Long ago there were these things called carousel projectors, machines with a projecting lens and a circular carousel on top that held many slides, or images. The carousel would project these images on a screen, and the images could be advanced one at a time with the push of a button. They were quite popular.

He said that he planted electrodes, sensors that detect electrical activity, in the subject's motor cortex, gave them a button with a cord to the projector, and told them to advance the carousel anytime by pushing the button. The idea was that the subject had a free choice, or free will, whether or when to advance the carousel to the next slide. However, unbeknownst to the subject, the button was a dummy that was not attached to the carousel at all. The cord from the button terminated under the rug. What really advanced the carousel was the amplified electrical signal from the electrode implanted in the subject's motor cortex. In other words, the carousel advanced only when the motor cortex of the subject's brain sent an electrical charge to the carousel to do so.

Dr. Walter said the results were astonishing. He said the subjects were startled because it seemed to them the slide projector was anticipating their decisions. They said just as they were about to push the button—but before they had decided to do so—the projector would advance the slide! He said, They were worried that if they pushed the button, it would advance the slide twice!

What we concluded from this experiment, continued the doctor, was that it was not the subject consciously deciding to advance the carousel; rather, it was the brain making a decision to advance it before the subject was aware of it—put another way, it was the subject's physical brain making decisions before the subject knew it! Indeed, he said, they concluded that free will is nothing more than a split-second veto power over an already-made decision by the physical brain.

Athena asked Dr. Walter if this was not a clear indication that decisions made by humans are brain- or materially, based.

Like Dr. Harlow before him, he paused long, looked at Athena, and said, A bold assertion that is probably true.

Near-Death Experience

Athena then said another experience that sheds light on whether human strategies to avoid the fear of death-work are near-death experiences. You may recall that Elpis defended religious afterlife against materialism and that Rhea was skeptical. They both said that they would discuss the issue as it pertained to near-death experiences. Elpis will start by defending an immaterial afterlife, followed by Rhea, who will argue for materialism.

I should say first that it is only natural that near-death experiences have become so emotionally debated. These powerful, intense, and highly personal experiences have become significant because medicine has blurred the boundary between life and death, which has caused people to rethink what it means to live and die.

Elpis began with the explanation that near-death experiences occur when someone has clinically died, or when their heart stopped beating, they stopped breathing, and their brain went silent, but then they are medically resuscitated and regain life, which sometimes happens with cardiac arrest in hospital emergency rooms. As medical technologies improve, more people are being brought back from death. Some who have spent hours with no breath or pulse buried in snow or submerged in very cold water, she continued, have made full, or nearly full, recoveries.

The testimonials of these people who have died and returned are quite eerie. They describe a sensation of floating up and viewing the scene around their unconscious body; they describe time spent in a beautiful, otherworldly realm; they talk convincingly about meeting spiritual beings like angels and being in the presence of a loving God, which they describe as a feeling of connectedness to all creation as well as a sense of transcendent love; they invariably describe encountering long-lost relatives and friends; and they often recall scenes from their youth. Universally, they describe their disappointment and reluctance at being called back from this magical realm into their body.

Elpis then said, Many believe near-death experiences prove there is a mind, or soul, that exists in some nonmaterial form independent of the body. For them, this offers escape from a cruel life that only ends in death and the possibility that people are more than meat. Certainly, Rhea, you may be critical of this perspective, but let me ask you, why have so many documented near-death experiences been the same? The testimonials described earlier tend to unfold in the same order. Why have so many people's near-death experiences been alike? There are just too many similar accounts of how humans have experienced death, verified by respected physicians, to ignore.

I understand it is impossible to obtain reliable data on what actually happens to people who felt their brains and bodies went elsewhere, but even if an afterlife isn't real, their sensations of having been there certainly are, which itself is significant.

Rhea thanked Elpis for her observations but said she remained skeptical. Rhea said, There is just too much evidence otherwise. Elpis is right in saying there is no reliable data on near-death experiences; indeed, studies have failed to find ironclad veridical, or not illusionary, perceptions from those who have died and returned. However, she continued, consider a few scientific facts. Medical scientists have long known that hypoxia—or oxygen shortage, which is common in cardiac arrest cases—often leads to confusion, disorientation, and hallucinations. This could be due to a variety of causes, including imperfect anesthesia or the body's neurochemical response to trauma. One study with rats showed their electroencephalograms spiked just before dying with an intensity that suggested their brain was more active than when they were awake. This could mean that the brain goes into a final, hyperactive spasm when its oxygen supply is cut, which comports with many physicians' observations that a hyperactive brain under the stress of approaching death often triggers massive hallucinations. It would seem then that near-death experiences are nothing more than the product of spasms of a dying brain.

Let me describe one remarkable near-death experience that supports this point of view. I mentioned the electroencephalogram, which is a sensor test that detects electrical activity in the brain using electrodes attached to the scalp. The brain's activity shows up as wavy lines on an electroencephalogram recording. I should mention that these recordings usually go flat within about twenty seconds of the heart stopping. Well, there is a case where a patient who went into cardiac arrest during surgery and was revived said they distinctly watched and heard the doctor sawing on them from high in the room. The patient's description of the doctor's actions was adamant and very accurate. However, when they later compared the patient's description with the doctor's activities, a different explanation emerged. The electroencephalogram showed that the patient's brain was active while the sawing procedure was being done. Even though the patient was partially dead, their still-active brain actually heard the saw. More importantly, there were numerous other things the doctor did when their electroencephalogram was flat that they could not recall. They could not recall them because they were dead and their brain was inactive. This supports the view that near-death experiences occur only when the physical brain is very much alive.

Rhea almost whimsically said, Humans are so interesting. They are forever claiming things exist, like God and near-death experiences, based on personal experience. Trying to disprove these kinds of assertions is like trying to rationally prove someone who claims to have seen a unicorn is wrong.

So, Rhea concluded, I remain skeptical about the veracity of other-world near-death experiences. The stories of Phineas Gage, Grey Walter's carousel, and near-death experiences demonstrate materialism, which itself means all is determined for humans, so their strategies to avoid the fear of death fail.

Determinism

Athena then thanked Elpis and Rhea for their explanations. She said, To repeat Rhea's assertion, if all is material, then humans are governed by necessary laws, which means all is determined. Perhaps the most famous proponent of determinism is the nineteenth-century French aristocrat and strict determinist and materialist Baron d'Holbach, with his book *Are We Cogs in the Universe?* I have asked Charon to bring the Baron before us.

The famous baron was calmly impressed with the gods and prepared to explain the reasons for his beliefs. He first said, Humans always act in accordance with necessary laws; their actions are never free. They are not free agents in any one instant of their life. They are necessarily guided in every step. He then read a passage from his book to support this view:

> Humans are born without their consent, their organization depends on others, their ideas come involuntarily, their habits are in the power of those who cause them to contract them-humans are necessarily modified by causes. Action is a result of the impulse they receive

either from the motive, from the object or from the idea. They do not act from their impulse, but rather from forces that modified their brain in a different manner.

Athena thanked the Baron for his explanation and asked him to stay, because Rhea was going to describe some of the consequences of his views.

Some Consequences of Materialism and Determinism

Rhea began by saying, If all is material and determined, there can be no mystical religions and no need for faith. Those who insist on believing in religious stratagems live in a strange existential tension. They try to deny what they know, thus perpetually living with the nagging doubt that they might be wrong. Indeed, it was the famous human religious thinker Reinhold Niebuhr who wrote that the great enemy of those with faith is doubt. These are the dreamers who get run over by a bus.

Further, if all is material and determined, then consciousness is a misnomer, no such thing exists, and the human psychologist Sigmund Freud was wrong. Consciousness is just the physical brain's electrical activity in response to numerous sources of input from the senses, and when the senses fail, there is no more consciousness. It turns out that humans, then, are just very sophisticated machines made of tissue and blood and nothing more.

Most significantly, however, if all is determined, Rhea continued, nothing matters. It does not matter what a person does because whatever they do was predetermined and they cannot change it. A person has no ability to alter their future with their mind because what the mind wills was determined beforehand.

The Baron said that Rhea was right, but he was troubled by the thought that his beliefs led to a state where nothing matters. He said he thought pretending things matter was better than throwing your hands up in nihilistic skepticism.

Rhea thanked the Baron and concluded with the observation that many human disciplines, including philosophy, psychology, art, and religion, that imagine those free immaterial states make more of it than there is.

Ways Humans Die

Hygeia took over and said, One disease that takes its time to kill humans is diabetes.

The Baron had been on his way out, but he paused when he heard this. He looked at Hygeia and said, It was diabetes that killed me. It is an awful disease that made me urinate all the time, I was always thirsty and hungry, I had blurry vision, plus numbness and tingling in my hands and feet, and I was always tired.

Hygeia asked the Baron to describe the disease.

The Baron said, Diabetes is a chronic, long-lasting health condition that affects how your body turns food into energy. The food you eat is broken down into sugar, or glucose, and released into your bloodstream. Normally your pancreas produces insulin that lets the blood sugar into your body's cells for use as energy, which reduces the amount of glucose in your body. However, with diabetes your pancreas does not produce enough insulin, so too much sugar stays in your bloodstream. Over time this causes serious health problems, like heart disease, vision loss, and kidney disease.

He said, There are two types of diabetes. Type one is caused by an autoimmune reaction where the body attacks itself by mistake. This stops the body from making insulin altogether. About 5 to 10 percent of people have this type. Its symptoms develop quickly, and it's usually apparent in children, teens, and young adults. Type two diabetes, which is the kind I died from, is when your body does not use insulin well and can't keep blood sugar at normal levels. About 90 to 95 percent of people have type two, which is usually diagnosed in adults.

The Baron then said, Millions of American adults have diabetes. It is the eighth leading cause of death in the United States, and it is the number one cause of kidney failure, limb amputations, and blindness. Unfortunately, there is no cure for diabetes, but losing weight, eating healthy foods, and being active helps. He said, I could have died from heart attack, stroke, or cerebral damage, but it was kidney failure that killed me. Once diagnosed, the life expectancy of a diabetic is about ten years. I was diagnosed with the disease at thirty-five and died at fifty, still a relatively young man. Hygeia then thanked the Baron, who left with Charon.

Athena asked whether humans' strategies to avoid their fear of death worked. The gods' conclusion was that if materialism and determinism were true, human strategies would appear to fail. They seem more like ways to make humans feel better about dying than accepting the stark reality of death itself.

CHAPTER 11
Third Heart Attack

A THENA SAID, REALIZING THEY WILL DIE IS AN IMPORTANT DIScussion for humans because the topic is what humans think when they are going to die. We have thoroughly discussed the strategies they use to avoid their fear of death and why they don't work. Now we will discuss how death looks to them when they stare it square in the face without strategies, rationalizations, or excuses. It is called "the existential slap" when they realize they are going to die.

Asclepius, god of health and medicine, told frightened Oscar, It looks like your number is up. He said that because Oscar had not changed his bad habits, he could die anytime from a third heart attack. He said it would happen quickly, kill him quickly, and could be triggered by any stressful physical or emotional event.

Putting on a courageous face, Oscar looked at Asclepius and said he still feared death, but he was now more fatalistic and, hesitatingly, prepared to die.

Jumpy Phobos, the god of fear, was heard to mumble, Of course, he has no choice.

Ominous Symptoms

Asclepius said, The truth is that Oscar already knew he was in trouble and that he could have a fatal third heart attack at any time because he had been experiencing the ominous warning signs of serious heart problems. If he walked up a flight of stairs—something most people do without thinking—he would get angina, shortness of breath, dizziness, nausea, and flulike symptoms. He had had his first heart attack at twenty-eight, when the doctors put in a stent, and a second heart attack at thirty-two, when the doctors performed a triple bypass. But there were new ominous symptoms that worried Oscar, including loss of appetite, increased weakness, labored breathing, changes in urination, and swollen extremities. He had been told these are signs of impending death.

Even though Oscar said he was prepared to die, his life had become a surreal kaleidoscope of vacillating contradictory thoughts and feelings. On one hand the old sense of dread and doom pervaded his life when morbid thoughts of death flooded his mind. He was terrified by the thought of his warm, live body buried lifeless deep in the cold, cold ground. His fear of death only brought him depression, helplessness, and the thought that nothing matters. He often thought of suicide. These were emotional reactions to his thoughts of death.

However, sometimes he would look at death pensively and be flooded with different thoughts and feelings. He would think about the fact that everyone dies, which brought him a sense of resignation and comfort because he realized the futility of worrying. He was not alone. He would think, It will happen so just accept it. This brought him a deep sense of relief that it would all be over soon. Clearly, Oscar's feelings about death were still intense but were now more personal because he was closer to it.

At age thirty-eight he felt he was too young to die. As his thoughts began to turn to the specter of sudden death, he became fearful of going back to the hospital because he feared that, once admitted, he might never return home.

Sudden Death

Thanatos, the arrogant god despised by all the female gods, said, There is a fine line between life and death. Humans die easily and suddenly in many ways. Indeed, their brain EEGs typically go flat within twenty seconds of their heart stopping. Most sudden deaths occur to the aged, diseased, or feeble, but sudden death also occurs in those under thirty-five, usually due to some heart abnormality. It can occur in males during some physical activity, like playing a sport, when their heart starts beating abnormally and uncontrollably with ventricular fibrillation.

Mortified, Oscar recalled his friend Benas Savickis, who died suddenly from a heart attack while playing basketball. It was then that Oscar realized that there had been some warning symptoms Benas mentioned, including wheezing, fainting, and dizziness, but these were nothing compared to the hart palpations, irregular heartbeats, and chest pain Benas experienced when he suddenly died.

The philosopher goddess Rhea said, Human philosophers have often written about sudden death. Cicero wrote that *death is daily close at hand, and because of the shortness of life, it is never far away*; Seneca wrote that *there are no rules to death; whatever can happen at any time can happen today*; and Marcus Aurelius that *you may leave this life at any moment; keep this possibility in your mind in all that you say or think.*

Oscar naturally began thinking more about life than sudden death.

Oscar Contemplating Life

Aloud, Oscar began ruminating on life and death. Pensively, he said that he had tried to live a full, worthwhile life, but ended up living a shallow, almost cowardly one. In an offhanded way, he said that partly because of this, he was getting tired of life. He said, It is just more of the same, like an old song played over and over. I have no real interests left or desired goals that make life interesting. I am getting ready to die.

The gods listened to Oscar with rapt interest, especially Hera, the goddess of women, marriage, family, childbirth, and hearth. She is everyone's favorite because she acts and thinks like a natural mother. She said, These words from Oscar make me sad. Because he is contemplating death, he has read some letters from young men solders to their parents, wives, and children to find out how others handled their impending death. These were young men who did not expect to survive the next day's battle—they are thoughts of young men expecting to die. Some were stoic, like the one who wrote that the *uncertainty of living ought to induce everyone to prepare for death.* Some were fearful, like the one who wrote, *I'll try to tell you how scared I am now, I wonder how I will make it, my luck seems to be running good for now, just hope it lasts.* One was courageous, observing, *There has been much to make life sweet and glorious, but death, while distasteful, is in no way terrible.* And a few were sadly practical, like the young man who wrote, *We can't live forever, I am not afraid to die, I just hate the thought of not seeing you again.* These comments had a profound impact on Oscar, who began thinking how these observations mirrored many of his thoughts.

Oscar had always wanted to be young again. It was a tactic he used to avoid the fear of aging and dying. It occurred to him that wishing he was young meant he had lived an unsatisfied, meaningless life. He said that because he had not done what he wanted to do in life, he was yearning to relive his life so he could. He realized that if he had lived a full, meaningful life, he would not have the desire to be young and relive his life because his life would have been everything he wanted—there would be no need to relive it. But then he asked himself why he would want to be a poor, miserable, unhappy youth again with little understanding of life.

With these thoughts, Hera said, Oscar is becoming wiser.

Attitude toward Death

Hera then said to Oscar, The world is as you make it, and the same goes for death—it is what you think it is. There are two different human attitudes toward death; I call them angry-resisting and serene-accepting ways of thinking. Angry-resisting people are so egotistically wrapped up with their lives they get mad when they die. They are the ones who think only of their careers and money and never stand back and take a broad look at their lives and ask, is this enough? Is something missing? They mourn their dying and feel sorry for themselves.

The serene-accepting kind see death differently. Certainly, they think of themselves and their aspirations, but at the same time are other-regarding. They also mourn their dying, but they think about all the good things they have enjoyed in their lives as well the good things left to enjoy. They rarely feel the need for more and are less inclined to wonder if they have missed something. They think of death as normal and just accept it serenely.

Oscar thought he wanted to be more like the serene-accepting kind.

Getting Older

Hera continued and said to Oscar, It is more than just your attitude toward death, it is also your attitude about getting older.

This caught Oscar's attention, because at thirty-eight, he was beginning to feel the effects of aging and the long, grueling battle with death. He looked at Hera and said that perhaps he should be thinking more about life than death, or how he ought to live.

Hera said, That is one of the wisest things you have said. It is a mistake to want to be young again or to thwart death, because aging and death are natural. It was your Stoic philosopher Marcus Aurelius who wrote that you should be content with your allocation of time.

Oscar began pondering aging. It occurred to him that lamenting getting older and regretting how he had lived was a waste of time because the past cannot be changed. He also thought about the pains of aging, like his aching joints, loss of strength and vitality, and illness. He recalled the many things he could no longer do, like run fast and make love late into the night, but then he thought about something Theodore Roosevelt quoted in his autobiography: *Do what you can, with what you've got, where you are.* But this seemed like little compensation for his squandered youth. He thought it sounded like resignation and a soothing platitude for getting old.

Athena, who had been listening to Oscar's thoughts, told Oscar they were misplaced. She said that he should listen to his human philosophers on aging. She said Cicero wrote that *old age is the last act of life, and, as at a play, if we find it boring, we ought to make our exit, especially if we have already had our fill*; Seneca admonished people to *cherish and enjoy old age because fruit tastes most delicious when the season is ending,* and *How nice to have outworn one's desires.* And Marcus Aurelius had the profound thought that *an educated attitude toward death does not find it superficial or disdainful; rather, simply awaiting it is one of the functions of nature.*

Oscar Begins Rethinking How to Live

Athena's comments made Osar think about what his thoughts would be when he knew he was going to die. He would not think about the size of his bank account, whether he knew the right people, or how luxurious his house was. Rather, he knew he would be thinking about all the people he knew in his life, like his wife Madeline and children Megan, Mehal, and Maurice, and his friends, including Benas. He would also think about his life challenges and accomplishments. Oscar began thinking more about accepting death and making the remainder of his life more meaningful.

Third Heart Attack

It was a cold, dark day in February when Oscar learned that his son Mehal had drowned. This unexpected shock stressed Oscar's already weakened heart, which brought on the ominous signs of an impending heart attack. Oscar knew the symptoms well: shortness of breath and unbearable crushing angina. He wasted no time and went directly to the hospital.

Hygeia and Asclepius were sure Oscar would die. They discussed how the average person often survives their first heart attack with proper medical care, and sometimes their second, but very few survive their third. It looked like Oscar was on his way out.

Oscar had his third heart attack in the hospital emergency room. He experienced the same physical pain and mental anguish, but because he was heavily sedated, the pain was less intense. But the mental experience was more real.

For Oscar it was déjà vu. The same surreal slow motion, the dimming lights, the black sack, and the dreamlike images of dead people he had known. However, it was different this time. In his dream state, he looked forward to the best parts of the dying experience. It was like watching the best parts of his favorite movie again. He relished the body separation, entering darkness and then entering light, which brought him that familiar sense of peace and well-being. It was the easy, comfortable, and pleasurable experience he knew. The doctors and nurses were surprised by the large smile on dying Oscar's face.

Oscar yearned to die and join his old beckoning friends, and he felt certain he was on his way when again he was yanked back into the ugly, brightly lit surgery room with strange people. The smile disappeared from his face as the pain and mental anguish returned. He was aggrieved at surviving and deeply distressed at knowing he would have to repeat the awful process another day.

The only reason he survived his third heart attack was because he had it in an emergency room; otherwise, he certainly would have died. The doctors pored over his medical record and did their usual tests. They saw he had a stent from his first heart attack and a bypass from his second. The tests indicated a heart valve had been seriously damaged during this third heart attack. The valve opening had narrowed, and the valve itself did not close completely, which allowed blood to flow backward reducing the forward blood flow. This in turn overloaded his heart, so they decided to install a new valve. The cardiac surgeon cut down the midline of Oscar's chest through the breastbone to reach his heart. He then carefully removed the diseased valve and replaced it with a mechanical one, which quickly turned Oscar's pale complexion pink.

Oscar barely survived his third heart attack, but he was now a different man. The experience had a profound impact on him. He began thinking about his wife and children, including Maurice, dead Mehal and daughter Megan, and began to look at death through new eyes. He also was left with a damaged heart that he knew would lead to the eventual cause of his death: congestive heart disease.

Grimy

Euphrosyne, goddess of cheer and mirth, excitedly said, Grimy is here!

Mean and opinionated Ares, god of chaos and war, was heard muttering, Here comes the dandy.

Grimy came in dressed as an angel because he had been to a costume party. He was obviously intoxicated, had a glass of wine in his hand and a big smile, and was jovial and full of cheer. He was just delighted to see everyone! He went straight to Oscar and fondly put his arm around him, saying, How wonderful it is to see an old friend. Grimy said, I have few old friends because, as a bounty hunter, they die quickly, except for you, Oscar.

Oscar was obviously irritated when he said, Good god, you again! He said that he was getting tired of living in Limbo where nothing matters. He was interested in dying. He said that he did not want to experience another heart attack and asked Grimy to harvest him now and guide his spirit to the next realm.

Grimy looked at Oscar's medical chart and consolingly told disappointed Oscar that because he had survived his third heart attack, he could not harvest him at this time. Grimy then returned to the party.

Ways Humans Die

Asclepius said, One of humanity's worst long-term wasting diseases is Parkinson's.

Mnemosyne, goddess of memory, pointed out, It is particularly awful for Oscar because his mother, Regina Uzgalis, died of it. Parkinson's is a neurological degenerative disorder that affects the brain and the central nervous system that affects the motor system. In the United States, about 60,000 new cases are diagnosed each year in persons older than sixty years of age. It affects about

50 percent more men than women. Its cause is unknown, but it occurs due to the lack of dopamine, a chemical neurotransmitter that coordinates movement, and the neurological transmitters become impaired or die.

There are three stages to the disease. Stage one is so mild that many attribute it to aging. It gets worse in the second stage, with tremors and muscle stiffness, and in the final advanced stage, sufferers may need a wheelchair and are sometimes bedridden, requiring full-time nursing. Parkinson's symptoms are usually described as early and late. Early symptoms include tremors, slowness of movement, stiff muscles, unsteady walk and balance, and coordination problems. Other symptoms often include speech changes, decreased facial expressions, depression, anxiety, drooling, memory problems, hallucinations, constipation, loss of smell, sleep disturbances (like restless leg syndrome), and pain. Its later symptoms are more ominous and often include trouble talking, difficulty sleeping, sometimes behavioral changes, worsening tremors and shaking, slowness of movement, rigid muscles, unsteady walk and balance, muscle twisting, spasms or cramps, and stooped posture. In its final stages, some critical bodily functions, like digestion, heart rate, blood pressure, and breathing, are often impaired.

With tears in his eyes, Oscar recalled his mother's suffering from the disease. He said that remembered when he was around five or six years old, she was in the kitchen trying to make dinner. He said he watched her struggling to hold the frying pan because she was shaking. She had difficulty setting the table for the family because she was so slow and unsteady, and in the end, she was gasping for breath due to pneumonia. He said it was in her bed when he watched the life go out of her pale face, which devastated him. With that Oscar went silent.

Panacea then said, There is no cure for the disease, and it only gets worse with time. She said most patients usually live ten to twenty years after being diagnosed, with the help of medications and sometimes surgery. Some medical treatments include levodopa, which is a natural chemical that converts to dopamine in the brain, and deep brain stimulation, where doctors implant electrodes in the brain that deliver electrical impulses that block the abnormal activity that cause the symptoms. Another treatment that delays the progress of the disease involves lifestyle changes. This includes increased exercise and a healthy diet. These are important because they hinder the two ways sufferers usually die, which are by falls (hence the need to maintain balance) and pneumonia.

The wise goddess of remedy Iaso said that she remembered Regina's death and that it still pained her to recall the angst it caused in young Oscar. However, looking at Oscar, she said, Like your mother, you now have your own life-ending disease to deal with. The rest of your life will be one long struggle with degrading congestive heart disease until it inevitably kills you. Let us now move on and discuss how you should live the rest of your life in order to make it as meaningful as possible. She said, Oscar is ready for this and sent him back to Limbo.

CHAPTER 12
Oscar's Epiphany

THANATOS STEPPED IN BRIEFLY AND REMINDED THE OTHER GODS that Oscar was not dead yet. He said, Recall that Hades and Grimy had resuscitated him and took him to Limbo, where he is now. He is alive and awaiting his fate. He said, Let's bring him here so we can ask him questions about his life.

Shortly, a surprised Oscar arrived.

Athena, a lesbian goddess wary of men, then looked at Oscar and said, Knowing your fate, let us now discuss Iaso's question on how you should have lived the rest of your life.

Heterosexual philosopher goddess Rhea, who loved men, said, Of course.

Euphrosyne, the goddess of mirth, was overhead chuckling about how her sister goddesses' sexual preferences affect their advice to humans like Oscar.

Athena told Oscar, This is a seminal time in your life, because your heart attacks made you ponder life's true meanings for a short time.

Oscar looked at Athena as if a truth had been revealed and said that each heart attack had caused him to ponder his existence.

Downcast, he said he knew he had lived a shallow life, that he had feared death, and that his strategies to avoid that fear had all failed.

Impressed with his honesty, Athena said, Of course different things give different people meaning, but there seem to be two necessary constants. The first is to be independent, self-directed, and free from others' judgments.

Euphrosyne chuckled again because she knew Athena wanted women to be free and independent from men. She also knew that Athena always emphasized the future and abhorred the past and present.

Practical Iaso spoke up and said, The other source of meaning in life comes when humans summon the courage to accept death.

Euphrosyne again chuckled because she knew that Iaso naturally emphasized the past.

Like someone who has just gained a brilliant insight to a problem, Athena exclaimed she had just realized that Oscar's life was very much like the fictional character Ivan Ilych, who was created by the great Russian writer Leo Tolstoy. She said, In Tolstoy's book *The Death of Ivan Ilych*, Ivan also had lived a very shallow life until he contracted a fatal disease. The book was about what he thought while dying and how those thoughts enabled him to discern what is important in life. She then told somewhat befuddled Oscar that she would explain how shortly.

What Constitutes a Meaningful Life

So, continued Athena, let us now discuss what constitutes a meaningful life, which is an important theme because it determines your happiness. At some point in their lives, most humans, while groping for meaning, think life is meaningless and nothing matters because they die. But this sets up a contradiction: they think life is meaningless, but they yearn for meaning. When you thought, because I die nothing matters, you had de facto made your life meaningless because you had given death primacy. The only solution is to ask yourself, why must my life have meaning? Why is it a problem if it does not? Why isn't it all right to live a pointless life? Most significantly, it really does not matter that it does not matter that your life had no ultimate meaning.

These wise words made Oscar think. He remembered how, after each of his heart attacks, when he was looking into the abyss, many things in his life became conspicuous. He realized he had not thought about money or how important he was, but rather about the people he knew and loved. He also thought about the fact that he would die and be nothing soon. Uncharacteristically, he had thought, So what! He thought ultimately it did not matter that he would die. With these ideas, Oscar's mind began to turn on what constitutes a meaningful life.

Athena, who was pleased with Oscar's thoughts, said. Let us expand on these initial ideas and break them down into what constitutes a meaningless and a meaningful life. I will begin with meaningless thoughts, actions, and circumstances, because they should be quickly rejected as negative influences.

Meaningless Life

Most people live life half-asleep, unwittingly compelled to do unimportant things. Because they never stop to contemplate life and death, they are chasing the wrong things. They think they are important because they are always in a hurry, as if they are running an imaginary race for meaning. Ironically, they think they have to run faster and faster to find it. These are the ones who suffer meaningless lives. A few of their self-defeating beliefs include, as previously mentioned, that nothing matters and that they must live in others' judgments.

Also previously mentioned, they ask themselves why they should bother looking for meaning because they will die and be gone soon. They think life is pointless, so they live like a bunch of sheep mindlessly obeying their master, the sheep dog, and the herd. They think because they die, rot, and become nothing, all they can do is live out their lives painlessly without trying to be special. They are the ones your famous musician Willie Nelson lampooned when he sang, "Turn out the lights, the party's over/They say that all good things must end…/ And tomorrow starts the same old thing again." They are also the ones who suffer from Baron d'Holbach's determinist views, because they think they have no free will. They think, if everything is determined, life is pointless, so why bother trying? This way of thinking robs any life of meaning and puts them in solitary confinement.

At this time Thanatos told Athena that Rhea would now discuss with Oscar some additional thoughts and actions that cause meaningless.

Rhea thanked Athena, looked at Oscar, and said, Living in others' judgments is another way to a meaningless life because it imprisons your mind and steals your imagination.

Oscar nodded with approval and said he had mentioned earlier that he thought letting society determine his success had only led him to a hollow, insincere life full of silent resentment and anger.

Rhea said, Yes, and some believe it is bourgeois business and professional classes' ideas and standards that are the most ruinous. They think it is this mediocre, town-living class—which is only one step up from farming peasants—that values wealth and freedom, and that does the most damage. She then told Oscar, The critics may be right in some of their accusations, but this rising bourgeois middle class is the first class in history to live and think independently from the upper royal and clerical classes. This has allowed them to value what they want, which has brought them meaning. Indeed, much of the upper classes' criticism is borne of jealousy.

Rhea continued, There are many other reasons people live meaningless lives, a few of which I will only briefly mention. Materialism is an empty goal; money does not bring meaning in itself, and the desire to get more is self-defeating. Thinking that things bring meaning is a mistake. Material things do not hug back, to which Platus reluctantly agreed. Rhea continued, Enduring meaning also does not come from who you know, prestige, power, or sensual pleasure because they are transient and unfulfillable. Certainly there are uncontrollable circumstances that make it harder to live a meaningful life, like war, illness, poverty, and racism, but not necessarily so.

So, Rhea said, now let us discuss the ways to think and act that lead to meaningful lives.

Meaningful Life

Panacea, the goddess of universal remedy, asked Oscar what he thought about what had been said.

Oscar, deep in thought on life and death, said he thought a prerequisite to a happy and meaningful life was to know that we make our own meaning, which is the opposite of living under others' judgments. He said he had come to realize that true meaning comes from within—that we find our own meaning in life.

Obviously amused, Panacea said, You sound just like the famous philosopher Ralph Waldo Emerson, who championed self-reliance.

Euphrosyne, the goddess of mirth, said she thought it was love that brought the greatest meaning to humans' lives. She said, It is the love, gentleness, tenderness, and comradeship between people that brings true happiness. Giving and receiving love is the only rational act, because it is love that always wins in the end.

Rhea said, It is people who give meaning to life.

This animated Oscar, who said he had mentioned earlier that after each of his heart attacks, when he was facing death, all he thought about were people, mostly his family and friends. He said he thought about Luke O'Sullivan, the poor young messenger boy at work who had revered him, and his own youngest son Maurice, who loved him.

Of course, Rhea said, loving others, having a kindred spirit, and interacting affectionately with others are the true stuff of meaning in life.

Rhea said, One often overlooked source of a meaningful life is simplicity, or to live simply. It seems most humans are only happy when they are involved in a variety of activities, but a few, usually due to profound thought, purposely live simple lives. They enjoy the small pleasures, or what the French call *petite bonheurs*, like singing, talking with a friend, laughing, dancing, or just walking through a forest. Which brings to mind the famous American Henry Thoreau, who famously wrote, *Simplify, simplify, simplify!* He was a proponent of living in nature, or with nature, which he did on Walden Pond. Nature calms, refreshes, and renews us; it is our true crucible to which we return when we die and become nature ourselves. Like Aristotle's acorn mentioned earlier, Rhea said, you should do and think the things that bring you purpose, because this naturally generates interest and meaning in life. Indeed, one reason to have goals is because they do just that.

Rhea continued, There are many other avenues to meaning that should be mentioned. Being industrious, expending effort, and facing and overcoming challenges are great sources of satisfaction and meaning. Acquiring knowledge is another way. Knowledge may bring confusing ambiguity, but it also engenders awareness and understanding, which are sources of meaning. To move beyond your ego and become useful, to have passion for something, and to seek adventure—whether it be travel or motorcycling—are all sources of meaning. The list of activities you can take up that can bring you meaning are endless, including going to college, competing in a sport, reading good books, starting a business, and writing.

Finally, let me just say life has no ultimate meaning. The only true and sure thing is that you will die. Everything else is a footnote, so humans should decide to live their lives as best they can in a way that brings them meaning. It is the only thing you can do.

Steve Jobs

Rhea then told Oscar he should know what famous American entrepreneur and businessman Steve Jobs said about life and death. Mr. Jobs, who had been at the cutting edge of technology with his fledgling company Apple Computer Company, died young at age fifty-six from pancreatic cancer. Some of his final thoughts were to always ask if this is your last day; to ask if you are satisfied with what you are doing; to be aware that when you die, you have nothing to lose; to know that your time is limited, so don't waste it; to listen to your own inner voice and not others' dogma; and to have the courage to follow your heart and intuition.

Perhaps his most ontologically poignant observations on death were that death is an inescapable destination we all share, and nobody wants to die, but must.

Dionysus's Party

Oscar was feeling overwhelmed with this flood of new knowledge when Grimy showed up and asked if he would like to go to a party. He told Oscar that in spite of his job, he felt like a friend who would like to see Oscar have some fun before he was gathered. Excitedly, he said, The party is at Dionysus's place, and everyone will be there.

Oscar was confused. He thought it odd to be going to a party when he was facing death, odd that the Grim Reaper asked him, and rather strange to think he would be partying with the gods. But, he thought, why not? So he said, Let's go!

When they got there, the party was in full swing. Nyx, Elpis, and Hypnos were drunk on wine and joyfully singing dirges; groaning Aphrodite was in the bedroom with Priapus having sex; Poseidon and Ares were wrestling in the kitchen; Hera and Thanatos were in a corner intensely debating feminism; and wise Athena was passed out in the recliner. It was a wild party. Dionysus welcomed Oscar, put his arm around him, gave him a glass of wine, and suggested he take Metis to bed, which Oscar eventually did.

As the evening progressed, Oscar noticed the personality differences between open and loving Euphrosyne—goddess of mirth who loved people and a party—and closed and guarded Mania, goddess of insanity and the dead, who was uptight, rude, and disliked people. He noticed how Euphrosyne's lively personality attracted people; she was the cynosure of the party, unlike Mania, who was either in an argument with someone or brooding in a corner. He marveled at how these two goddesses' outlooks on life affected their circumstances and happiness. It occurred to him that when you value people, like Euphrosyne, your life naturally has a deeper meaning, whereas when you don't, like Mania, life can be quite mean. Oscar thought having a meaningful life was not that complicated. Clearly those who are people-oriented live better lives.

On their way back to Limbo, Oscar told Grimy that he had a wonderful time drinking, talking with the gods, and making love to Metis at the party. He thanked him for the invitation.

The Tolstoy Test of Values

After a few boring days in Limbo, Apollo, the prescient god of sun and healing, visited Oscar. He said that Athena had asked him, because he could see the future, to explain her earlier comment about Oscar's life being very much like fictional character Ivan Ilych, who had also lived a very shallow life until he contracted a fatal disease. Athena had said that it was only when facing inevitable death that Ivan was able to discern what was important in life. Apollo then said, The reason Athena mentioned this to you was because she wanted you, and all humans, to be aware of what she calls the Tolstoy test of values.

It is a simple mind experiment, Apollo continued, in which you project yourself ahead to your deathbed. From that mindset, knowing that you will be dead and gone shortly, ask yourself what is important in life. The perspicuity of your answers will startle you. When you know you will soon be gone forever, what is meaningful in life quickly becomes crystal clear.

Excited, Oscar said, Yes, let's do it. He began imagining what he would think when he was eventually harvested.

After a time, Oscar looked at Apollo with new eyes, as if he had been awakened. Oscar said that all the things he used to value, like money, position, and pleasure, quickly became irrelevant. He said he did not wish he had spent more time working. He said the only things he could think about were the people he had known in his life, in particular the ones he loved. He said, It seems when we think we are going to live forever, we indulge in meaningless trivia, but when we think about our imminent demise, what is important emerges like a photograph being developed. Surprised, Oscar said, Anyone who wants to know how to live a meaningful life should do this experiment. It will change their lives like it has mine.

Encouraged, Apollo then asked Oscar if he would like to know the exact day and time he would be taken.

An alarmed Oscar exclaimed, Absolutely not! It is one thing to know I am in Limbo, and in general that I will be taken, but quite another to know when. Knowing when you die takes all the mystery out of living, and it is the mystery that keeps life interesting and worth living.

The Necessity of Accepting Death in Order to Live a Better Life: Reprise

It was then that Mnemosyne, goddess of memory, told Oscar she was not as wise as Athena and Rhea, so she had remained mostly quiet, but she thought she had something important to say because it related to Oscar's memory, or what he already knows. She told Oscar that earlier he had learned why humans fear death, that to know death is to know life, and of the need to accept and practice death. She apologized if her comments were repetitious and somewhat rambling, but she wanted to remind him of the need to accept death because he had not realized the importance of it earlier. She told Oscar, It is only when you accept your demise that you learn how to live. Recall the famous human philosopher Seneca's admonition to be like *the man who finds joy in living in spite of death.* It seems that the people who are afraid of living are most fearful of death, whereas those who love living are not.

Mnemosyne then told Oscar that the gods had not mentioned that accepting death comes easier to some than others. She said, There are two human, often contradictory, views of human nature. The nature ones believe humans are a product of nature and its instincts, like the psychologist Sigmund Freud. The nurture group, like Rousseau, think humans are a product of society or civilization. It really does not matter which camp you fall in; the point is that those who think in natural and instinctual terms accept death more readily, whereas those who think society forms humans' character prefer to seek ways to overcome death.

Mnemosyne then talked about the reasons Rhea had emphasized accepting death. She began by paraphrasing Mitch Albom's book *Tuesdays with Morrie*. She said that Morrie believed most humans live as if they are sleepwalking. They don't experience the world fully because they are half-asleep and do things automatically, thinking they have to. But when they truly realize they are going to die, they see everything differently. They no longer worry about the future, and they stop creating strategies to avoid thinking about death, which allows them to focus on living. The natural result is they live fuller and happier lives.

If you think about it, Oscar, Mnemosyne continued, your death is no big deal. Only your imagination makes it important. You, like most humans, think your lives are significant and living is normal, but you fail to understand your life is really insignificant and being dead is the norm. Indeed, you have spent the last thousand years being insignificantly and non-existently "dead." But it is not so bleak as that, because ontologically you will always be part of something. Ultimately, you do not go away, and you do not become nothing; rather, you just rearrange yourselves as other parts of nature's patterns. You become parts of everything else. You become other people, animals, earth, rocks, air, and water. There is nothing evil, sinister, wrongful, or fearful in being rearranged; it is just part of one large evolving process. If you can see this, your deaths become far more intimate and acceptable, and less fearful.

Death and Courage

It was here when Ares, god of courage and war, told Oscar that it was not enough to know you die, you must also have the courage to accept it. Indeed, the famous human author Ernest Hemingway's observation that *the coward dies a thousand deaths and the brave man once,* should be the coward, who fears death, dies a thousand deaths, whereas the courageous one, who accepts death, dies once.

Ares said, Many human philosophers have touched on this need for courage. Cicero observed that he either wished for death, or, at any rate, cease to fear it, and that *the man without the fear of death has secured a valuable aid toward a happy life.* Epictetus wrote, *We cannot escape death, but we can escape the dread of it, that the source of all human evils is not death but rather the fear of death,* and *When events are not in our power, like death and pain, we fear-face them with confidence.*

Knowing that he had faced certain death from a heart attack, Oscar began thinking more about his life. He recalled that he had been tired of his cowardly, shallow life and decided he did not want to leave this world in a state of fright. With this, plus Athena's earlier advice that most humans are like a flock of sheep blindly following the herd's instincts, Oscar began to understand what was important. He thought, We fear standing alone, and the solution is to have courage, to become self-reliant, independent, self-directed, and to ignore societal norms. Oscar recalled Athena's comments: I should have faith in myself, face up to the real world, and look to myself for strength.

Oscar's Epiphany

This was a momentous time in Oscar's life. His mind had ranged through a variety of life-changing issues that had touched his soul, which caused him to change his view of existence. It was a watershed time in his life, when his mind went in another direction. The way it went was to embrace his death because it was inevitable, and with that he began to do what he could to get the most out of his remaining time alive—to live a more meaningful life.

It was like being jolted by 1,000 watts of electricity that enlivened him, made him more aware, more thoughtful, and even a bit wise. His first electric reaction was to be glad he was alive and for the first time enjoy his senses—eyesight, hearing, and touch. To just exist, even in Limbo, awed and excited him. For the first time, he marveled at his brain and how it allowed him to think about so many profound, varied, and interesting things. For the first time, he studied with awe his earthly environment, including the people, institutions, and nature. He was particularly fascinated with his body and spent most of a day studying his hand. He thought, What a remarkable appendage, and wondered how and why it came about. For the first time, he pondered his emotions and wondered why he had them. Oscar's world became a kaleidoscope of deep thoughts and observations that stilled and calmed his soul.

After months of solitary contemplation, Oscar observed, There are many things that bring meaning to life, but there seem to be a few key ones. The first is health. Aghast, he realized how he had taken his health for granted and indulged in bad habits, like overeating and smoking. He wished he had resolved to develop healthy habits in order to help his body give him the time to get the most out of what remained of his life.

Oscar thought about other key aspects of life, like his wife, children and friends. He recalled how he had romanced and fallen in love with Madeline Walsh, how she had begged him to marry her, and how much he had resisted because he did not want the obligations and burdens a family and children bring. He thought about how he finally relented, married Madeline, started a family, and spent a good part of his life resenting having to support it. Thinking this way made Oscar feel like a fool. He thought, What an awful way to think. He thought how marriage had tested him and caused him to learn more about himself, how he had learned to accommodate and respect another person, to compromise, to set and pursue worthy common goals with another, and to establish common values. He thought to himself that if he had never married, he would have lived a solitary and lonely life without these lessons. For the first time in his life, he realized how lucky he had been to marry such a wonderful, beneficent woman with whom he shared his heart and life. He thought Hera was right—he was lucky Madeline married him.

Oscar's thoughts then turned to his children. With Madeline, he had made three; Megan, Mehal, and Maurice. From his new perspective, it embarrassed him to realize how little he had valued them. He had disliked his rebellious daughter, Megan, and had repressed the memory of Mehal, who had drowned, and he winced at how he had spurned the affection of his youngest son, Maurice.

Hera, goddess of marriage and family, listened to Oscar's thoughts with interest, and then told Oscar, If you want to have complete responsibility for another human, if you want to learn how to love, and if you want to bond in the deepest way, have children. It is not easy raising children because they can be rebellious, they might not like you, and they eventually leave, but that is the price you pay when you create them. Unfortunately, it has taken you a long time to realize this, but I suppose it is better late than never.

Prescient Apollo then added that Oscar was lucky to have come to this realization now. He said, Your son Mehal and grandson Lukas died long ago, Maurice died from amyotrophic lateral sclerosis soon, Megan died from influenza, and Madeline died from Alzheimer's, all before you die.

Speechless and obviously disturbed, Oscar looked at Apollo and said that his entire family dying before he did made him feel alone in the world.

Hera then reminded Oscar how he used to think family was a waste of time, how he thought he would waste the best young part of his life supporting a family. She pointed out that when he left for Limbo, his family became more important. It was the only firm ground he could stand on. She said, The love and caring of your family is unique because you know others are looking out for you. Nothing else gives you that, not money or fame.

Oscar realized how he had lived a dull, uneventful life and missed some of life's most profound things, like the love of family. He asked Hera if she would please hug his wife and children wherever they were, and she said she would try.

Oscar's thoughts then turned to his old friends, and he told Hera how these loving relationships had made life worth living. He said he greatly missed his best and oldest boyhood friend, Benas Savickis, who had died young from a heart attack. He reminisced about his youth with Benas knocking about Palanga together. Obviously pained, Oscar then described the break with another of his oldest friends, Domas Meka, because of some money Domas thought Oscar owed him. Good grief, Oscar exclaimed, a lost friendship over a few paper dollars! Oscar then asked Hera if she would go to Janina Meka, Domas's wife, to express his remorse and give her whatever he owed Domas.

Hera told Oscar that she could not pay anyone with human money, but she would try to find Janina and tell her his feelings.

It was then that Rhea and Oscar started talking philosophically. Oscar said he was ashamed of his past character; it was like he was another person. He said he should have thought deeper about profound issues, like death, family, society, forgiveness, and what constitutes a meaningful life, instead of wasting his life worried about trivial things like money, career, aging, and especially the fear of dying. Oscar's face lit up as if he'd had an epiphany, and he said he now knew how much richer his life would have been on earth if he had overcome his fear of death. He then said he should have discerned important life goals and thought more about what values to embrace. He wished he had understood the difference between happiness and meaning, because many sources of happiness are fleeting, like a mirage, but true meaning endures, which itself brings a state of satisfaction.

Instead, Oscar continued, I was a shallow person who was preoccupied with how I looked, who I knew, where I lived, how to get money, and where to find the next sensual pleasure. He said he was totally self-absorbed, prideful, and pretentious, driven by juvenile emotions like anger, jealousy, envy, and lust. Oscar paused a bit, and then looked at Rhea. At least I came to the realization that there is no Heaven, he said. It occurred to me that imagining any afterlife, like being in Heaven, was just one of my many strategies to avoid the fear of death, and this is one I overcame.

Ways Humans Die

Hygeia had a few comments on another way humans die. Amyotrophic lateral sclerosis, or ALS, once commonly known as Lou Gehrig's disease, is an awful way to die. *Amyotrophic* comes from the Greek word that means "without nourishment to muscles"; *lateral* means "to the side" and refers to the location of the damage cause by the disease in the spinal cord, and *sclerosis* means "degenerative scaring or hardening," which refers to the hardening nature of the spinal cord.

This caught Oscar's interest, because his youngest son, Maurice, had suffered and died from it.

Hygeia went on, ALS is a rare neurological progressive disease that affects the nerve cells responsible for controlling voluntary muscle movement. It is the deterioration and death of motor neurons that gradually stop sending messages to the muscles, which begin to weaken, twitch, and atrophy. There are three kinds of ALS: hereditary, called familial; nonhereditary, called sporadic; and one that targets the brain, called ALS dementia. It usually occurs between ages fifty-five and seventy-five and afflicts white men more than Hispanics and women. Like Parkinson's, the cause of ALS is unknown.

The early symptoms of ALS include muscle twitches and weakness, cramps, stiffness, slurred speech, and difficulty swallowing, which causes weight loss. The first sign of ALS is usually in a hand or arm that has difficulty functioning, like the inability to button a shirt. Sometimes sufferers trip or stumble. As the disease progresses, muscles become increasingly weak, and moving, speaking, and breathing become more difficult. In its late stage, the sufferer becomes immobile. They cannot stand, walk, get out of bed, or use their hands and arms. There is also constant, unremitting, chronic coughing because the lack of physical mobility decreases fluid intake, which results in shallow breathing and thickened secretions. Their coughing is an effort to clear their airway.

ALS is treated with medicines that control its symptoms, physical therapy, nutritional support, and breathing support with ventilation. These treatments can slow the progress of ALS, but they do not cure it. The disease is always fatal.

Sufferers die from ALS when their brain loses its ability to initiate and control voluntary muscle movements. Gradually, all voluntary muscles are affected, and individuals lose their strength and the ability to speak, eat, move, and even breathe. In the final stage of ALS, sufferers usually require a ventilator to live, which sometimes causes fatal pneumonia. The final cause of death for most people with ALS is respiratory failure, usually within three to five years of when the symptoms first appear. They die by suffocation.

Oscar listened to Hygeia's description of ALS in silence because he had watched his Maurice die a painful death from it. Distressed, Oscar recalled how awful it was to watch.

Hygeia said, If you humans want to live a meaningful life, do the Tolstoy test of values thought experiment and accept the reality that you die. Then she said, next Asclepius will describe some other ways humans die.

CHAPTER 13

How Humans Die

It was about this time when Oscar, who was talking with Thanatos and Asclepius, the gods of death and health, said that he expected to die an awful death due to his heart attacks. However, he said, other ways to die have been mentioned, and I would like to learn more about them.

Thanatos said, Humans die in many ways—from bad habits, like smoking, and due to circumstances, like pollution and war. Generally, however, humans die due to four sources: God, nature, other humans, and animals.

He went on, To answer your question, Asclepius and I will take you to meet some people who are in their final throes of dying from different causes. I have asked Chronos, god of time, to help us. He can take us back in time and through space to observe both the archaic and the contemporary ways humans die. However, be aware, Oscar, Thanatos continued, some of these ways are messy and gruesome, and these visits will be emotionally charged. You will be talking with some distraught people who are about to die.

The Ways Humans Die

Asclepius said, We have described ways to die from illnesses like heart disease, cancer, and Parkinson's Some means of death happen quickly and painlessly, like when you break your neck, and others slowly with intense pain, like cancer. Each of the ways damages some part of your body that can lead to death; however, the ultimate and universal underlying physiological cause of death from all illnesses is lack of oxygen. To live, you humans need oxygen, and when you don't get it, you die. All of the illnesses that lead to death that have been and will be described in some way kill you by depriving your body of oxygen.

Your brain and heart are particularly sensitive to the lack of oxygen. Without oxygen, the heart fails within four minutes and cannot be resuscitated. Your brain can continue for up to six minutes after your heart stops, but then it begins to die. When your heart and brain are dead, you are dead.

Let us begin by describing a few ways God kills humans.

By God

Influenza

Asclepius took Oscar to an intensive care unit, or ICU, at the hospital. They started talking with a very sick young woman who was dying from influenza. She was barely awake and suffering from a high fever, severe aching, and catarrh, or the excessive discharge or buildup of mucus in the nose or throat, which is usually due to inflammation of the mucous membrane. Oscar was emotionally affected at the sight of her because Megan, his daughter, had died of influenza.

Asclepius explained, Influenza is a highly contagious viral infection of the respiratory passages that often occurs as epidemics. There are four types of the influenza virus—A, B, C, D—and it is the B virus that primarily affects humans. The doctors treated her with fluid and anti-inflammatory pain relievers, and she is on a ventilator, but she has not responded. She is dying.

Oscar went closer to her and asked her name. Barely audibly, she said, Tricia. She had this ashen, supplicating, forlorn look that unsettled Oscar. It was the same look Megan had given him just before she died.

Asclepius told Oscar she would be dead before nightfall. He said, The influenza virus has triggered severe inflammation in her lungs, which is rapidly leading to respiratory failure. Even with the respirator, her lungs cannot transport enough oxygen for her body.

COVID-19

Asclepius then took Oscar to another ICU ward overflowing with patients suffering from the current respiratory disease epidemic, COVID-19. Oscar was nauseated by the loud coughing and wheezing. Asclepius told Oscar, These unfortunate people are suffering from this viral infection and are experiencing high fever, chills, fatigue, aches, and headaches. Even with rest, medications, and ventilators, many will die from the disease if it damages a major organ like the lungs, heart, kidneys, liver, or brain.

Pneumonia

They then went up a floor and entered a smaller ward where patients were suffering from pneumonia. Oscar walked over to one patient and asked what his name was.

Laboriously, leaning forward while coughing up a bloody mucus, he managed to say Jack, and then he fell back. A female nurse, who had overheard Oscar, came over and said Jack had developed pneumonia due to his COVID-19 infection. She said, He has a high fever, sweats and chills, shortness of breath, and rapid, shallow breathing. He winces every time he coughs because it gives him sharp, stabbing chest pains.

Asclepius thanked the nurse and then told Oscar, Pneumonia is a particularly gruesome way to die. It is lung inflammation caused by a bacterial or viral infection in which the air sacs fill with pus that sometimes becomes solid. It can affect both lungs, one lung, or only certain lobes. In spite of the antibiotics, cough medicine, fever and pain relievers, and ventilator, both of Jack's lungs have been infected. Jack is struggling to breath, his body is starved for oxygen, and he will succumb to asphyxiation within a few days.

Infection

In another room Asclepius and Oscar encountered a man who was comatose. Oscar asked his nurse why the man was ill, and she said, His name is Arnas, and he is dying from an infection.

Asclepius told Oscar, Infection is the invasion and multiplication of bacteria, viruses, or parasites in the body. Historically many people died from infections, but antibiotics had changed that.

The nurse then said that they had done all they could, including rest, increased fluid intake, and an antibiotic pump, but Arnas had not responded. She said, We are doing our best to make him comfortable, but he is still suffering greatly, even in his comatose state, from a high fever, chills and sweats, constant coughing, a sore throat, shortness of breath, and nasal congestion.

Asclepius told Oscar that most people with severe infections die one of two ways. If the infection is due to bacteria that entered an area without a blood supply, such as a gunshot wound, gangrene occurs, which produces toxins that release gas that cause tissue death and often the need for amputation. This is a life-threatening condition. The other way is by sepsis, a common killer in hospitals.

The nurse said that Arnas was in the last stages of sepsis. She said, The infection infused bacteria into his bloodstream, which released chemicals that have triggered inflammation throughout his body and damaged his lungs, urinary tract, skin, and gastrointestinal tract. With these organ failures, we expect Arnas to die anytime.

Asclepius then said, Let us now look at some ways nature kills humans. Certainly, earthquakes, hurricanes, and forest fires kill many humans, but let us look at hypothermia and immolation. Chronos, the god of time, is now here because he can transcend time and space to show us humans who are suffering from these maladies.

By Nature

Hypothermia

Chronos, who was a slow, learned old man, said, I am going to show you a young Hawaiian woman named Maile who is about a mile off the west coast of the island of Kauai in the Pacific Ocean. She was swimming when a strong current swept her out to sea.

Suddenly Oscar and Asclepius saw an afraid and panicking Maile at sea struggling to stay afloat.

Asclepius said, Hypothermia is when the body cools. The average human body temperature is 98.6 degrees Fahrenheit, and if it drops below 95 degrees, you become hypothermic. As you can see, Oscar, Maile is displaying all the symptoms of a cooling body: shivering, exhaustion, inability to think clearly, and confusion. If she could somehow get warmth—including recirculated, warmed blood at the hospital—her chances of survival would be good, but it looks like her body temperature has dropped too far. If so, many of her organs, especially her heart, nervous, and respiratory systems, will fail, bringing death.

Worried, Oscar asked Asclepius and Chronos if they could help her, and they said absolutely not. The Fates—especially Clotho, who spins destinies—do not like it when we meddle in their designs, Chronos said. She is too far gone, and she will die shortly from drowning due to hypothermia.

Immolation

Asclepius said, One excruciatingly painful way for humans to die is from immolation, or being burned alive. They can be destroyed by fire in many ways, including a forest fire and a nuclear bomb, although the later vaporizes quickly, so there is less pain. Immolation is painful because nerves are burned, so the immolated feels until they lose sensation in the burned areas. However, they usually die from inhaling toxic combustion products, hot air, and flames. These bring shock, which kills them long before the fire burns them up.

Chronos then showed Oscar and Asclepius a Buddhist monk named Chodha who was self-immolating in Lhasa, Tibet, to protest Chinese rule. The sight and smell were disgusting, horrid, and ghastly to Oscar. The monk's body was making a sizzling sound like a steak on a frying pan, and the smell was nauseating. It was sweet, putrid, and steaky, like leather being tanned over a flame. It got worse as he continued to burn. He began smelling like burned beef, hair, and flesh. There was a coppery metallic smell from his iron-rich blood along with the eyewatering scent of acrid, melted plastic. When the flames finally subsided, his corpse was black, but his internal organs were visibly intact due their high fluid content. When a couple of monks tried to pick up his burned corpse, sheets of his skin sloughed off their hands.

By Humans

Looking at Oscar and Chronos, Asclepius then said, Let us look at some ways humans kill humans. The famous human political scientist Thomas Hobbes once wrote that man is a wolf to man, and these ways of dying are good examples. These gruesome ways to die are usually done to execute or torture people; the first two, flaying and cutting, are particularly morbidly cruel.

Flaying

Chronos took Asclepius and Oscar to medieval Europe and showed them a man being flayed for impiety. Flaying, also known as skinning, is a slow and painful way to die in which the skin is removed from the body. They saw a man lying on a table running with red blood. He was screaming in pain because half of his skin had been cut off. The executioners were using their sharp knives to methodically skin him. The areas where his skin had been removed were bright red and oozing with blood.

Asclepius said, He will most likely die from shock due to exsanguination, or massive blood loss, or from the loss of body fluids, hypothermia, or infection. With this torture, death can occur in a few hours or a few days after being flayed. The best this man can hope for is an early death.

Cutting

Cronos then took them to sixteenth-century Qingdao, China, and showed them a grotesque-looking young man who was awash in blood because he had lost many body parts. He was writhing in great pain because he had lost some skin, a hand, a leg, his nose, an eye, and some fingers. There were even a few internal organs hanging out, which his tormentors were busily cutting up. Asclepius said that he was being tortured by cutting, or ling-chi, also known as death by a thousand cuts. He said, They just keep cutting him to pieces until he dies, usually from loss of blood, decapitation, removal of a major organ, or a stab to his heart. Like flaying, it is a long, slow process of punishment and lingering death.

Asclepius asked Chronos if he would take them to a few penitentiaries and places of execution so he could show Oscar a few more recent ways humans kill humans.

Hanging

Chronos first took them to San Quentin, a penitentiary near San Francisco, California. He showed them a young Black man about to be hanged in the execution chamber. Asclepius said, Hanging is death due to suspension by the neck. There was a rope around the man's neck, with a big knot by his ear. Suddenly the floor opened below him, and he dropped until the rope yanked his neck. Asclepius said, They die immediately if their neck gets broken or are slowly strangled by asphyxiation if it does not.

Guillotine

Chronos then took them to The Palace de la Révolution in 1793 France to watch the execution of a royal by the guillotine. The guillotine is a strange-looking device that suspends a very sharply angled blade high in the air and has a hole to secure a human neck. When the blade is dropped, the victim is decapitated. The death is quick and painless because the blade immediately severs the nerves between the spinal cord and brain, but leading up to it is excruciatingly fearful.

They watched the horrified royal slowly ascend the steps to the platform as everyone, including his executioners, looked on. The crowd was loud and demanded death, and some grotesquely carried severed heads atop pikes. Futilely, the royal resisted when the executioners forcibly strapped him to a flat board, lifted it, and then shoved his body forward so his neck was in the hole below the blade. There, the royal could gruesomely see many other severed heads in the basket below. He knew that his head would shortly join them when it separated from his body. The unfortunate royal had to wait an anguished moment for the blade to drop. With everyone watching, he heard the blade begin to fall and felt the hard steel against his neck while the crowd cheered. Most doctors say the victim loses consciousness within four seconds of decapitation, and the brain dies within one minute; however, some assert that the victim is alert up to thirty seconds after decapitation.

Guillotining was thought to be a humane way to die because it was so quick and painless, but the torture of the crowds, the anticipation, and the fear make it cruel.

Oscar said it was awful to watch.

Firing Squad

Next, Chronos took them to a military outpost where a deserter was about to be executed by a firing squad, a common form of military execution. He was a pale-looking young man who had been blindfolded and tied to a post. There were about eight or nine soldiers lined up about twenty feet away with their rifles aimed at either the heart or brain of the young man. A sergeant ordered fire, and there was instantly a din of gunfire as their firearms simultaneously went off, a fusillade of bullets penetrated his body, and the young soldier slumped to the ground dead. Asclepius said that it was an instant, painless death because the gunshots hit vital organs, which immediately ceased to function.

Sedatives

Asclepius said, The modern way humans execute other humans is with sedatives. A sedative is a drug prescribed for its calming or sleep-inducing effect, although it can also slow breathing and lower blood pressure and heart rates to dangerous levels. Iaso described it earlier as the drug doctors usually prescribe to end life for dying persons under Oregon's Death with Dignity Act because it quietly puts them to sleep and stops their bodily functions. It is the lethal overdose of a sedative, usually 500 milligrams of midazolam, that humans now use to kill because it quickly stops the condemned person's breathing.

Finally, Asclepius said, let's look at a few ways animals kill humans.

By Animals

Mauling

Chronos took Oscar and Asclepius to the Masai Mara National Park in Kenya, where they immediately saw a tourist being mauled by a lion. She had strayed from her hotel in the evening, which is the lions' hunting time. Asclepius said, To be mauled is to be killed by an animal, often by being ripped apart by their claws and fangs. Different animals maul in different ways. A bear, for example, tends to grab you by your neck and shake you, whereas a lion bites your neck in order to collapse your trachea, or windpipe, and suffocate you. Or it might violently bite and shake your spine to break it so you can't run away. Mauling can kill you many ways, including through suffocation, loss of blood, or loss of a vital organ. Generally, a bite to the neck or throat kills quickly.

Asclepius asked the woman who had recently been mauled what it was like. Obviously disturbed, the woman described it graphically. She said it was a surreal experience and that she was lucky to be alive. She said the lion's weight was immense as it forced her head into a twisted, crouching position. She said she felt the lion's hot breath on the back of her neck as its jaws closed around her scalp, dragging her head down close to the ground. She said she could feel its fangs chewing on the back of her head. She only survived because a perimeter guide shot the lion, and she was airlifted to a hospital in Nairobi, where she spent months recuperating.

Asclepius then said, We described how humans die from poisoning earlier, like from a snake, so let us finish with death by constriction, by a snake.

Constriction

Finally, Chronos took Oscar and Asclepius to the Amazon River in Brazil to watch a human as he was being constricted by an anaconda. Asclepius said, To be constricted is a strange way for you humans to die—to have a large snake coil tightly around you and squeeze with six pounds of pressure per square inch, or about the same pressure in a bicycle tire, until you die. It used to be thought that constriction caused death by asphyxiation, but it really kills by stopping the flow of blood inside you.

Chronos then took them to see Pedro, a former river guide, who had almost been killed by an anaconda's constriction. Oscar asked him what it felt like.

He said, the seventeen-foot snake attacked me with frightening speed, sank his curved teeth into my skin, whipped his slimy body around me, and dragged me to the bottom of the river. The pressure was tremendous, my windpipe was clamped shut, and I thought my eyeballs would pop out. I did not know if I would be able to draw another breath—I thought I was a goner. I learned later that constricting snakes, like the anaconda, use their prey's heartbeat to decide when it is safe to stop constricting. I think I survived because I had violently grabbed the snake's head and had a strong heartbeat. The snake decided to look for another victim and let me go. Pedro said that it was a frighting experience and that he was grateful to be alive.

Then Asclepius and Chronos said goodbye to Oscar and left him with Hypnos, the god of sleep, was going to discuss the relationship between sleep and death.

Death and Sleep

Hypnos, a very witty god, said, the shorter your sleep, the shorter your life. It is rarely published, but it's well known in medical circles that the lack of sleep leads to heart disease, dementia, diabetes, and cancer, to name a few ailments. With heart disease—such as yours, Oscar—lack of sleep causes the sympathetic nervous system to be in permanent fight-or-flight mode, which increases blood pressure, which in turn causes calcification of arteries. Indeed, those who are forty-five years or older and who sleep less than six hours a night are twice as likely to have a heart attack or stroke in their lifetime. Lack of sleep is a significant cause of many fatal diseases, and heart attack and stroke are the leading culprits.

But the relationship between sleep and death is even more profound. With no sleep, you quickly die. Perhaps the best example of this, continued Hypnos, is your fellow mortal Michael Corke.

Michael Corke

Hypnos said, In 1991 forty-year-old music teacher Michael Corke started to develop difficulty sleeping. He appeared to be in good health, but it was soon obvious he had something more than insomnia—he just could not sleep. Within a few months, his lack of sleep began causing physical and mental deterioration. He developed problems with balance, had trouble walking, started displaying signs of dementia, and occasionally would lose touch with reality and hallucinate. He was admitted to a hospital, at which time he was unable to communicate. He could no longer perform simple tasks like showering and getting dressed. His decline was rapid and pervasive.

At first the doctors could not figure out what was wrong with him. However, they soon discovered that even in his "sleep," when he closed his eyes and appeared to be sleeping, measurements of his brain activity found that his brain never did fall asleep. It was then that the doctors realized he was suffering from a recently recognized disease called fatal familial insomnia, now called fatal insomnia because not all cases are hereditary.

With this disease, sleep becomes progressively disrupted until patients experience little or no sleep, which inevitably brings death. Michael Corke was no exception. He had not slept for four months when he was admitted to the hospital, and after two more months he died. People like Michael Corke die when they have been awake for six months.

Death and Emotions

Hypnos then said that Phobos, a sadistic god who delights in human misery, had something to say about death and emotions.

Irritated by Hypnos's derisive introduction, Phobos asked Oscar what humans felt when they were old and preparing for departure.

All Oscar could say was fear.

Phobos said certainly, but there are many more emotions they experience, like trepidation, depression, desire, regret, and anger. There are also opposite emotions they experience, like acceptance, welcoming, wonder, and calmness. Their emotions are often a consequence of their circumstances. A young person may experience fear and anger because they are dying young, whereas an older dying person may feel calm and welcoming.

My point, continued Phobos, is that these are mostly emotional and not intellectual responses to dying. I delight in human pain and fear, and endeavor to emphasize humans' emotional response to dying because it exacerbates their fear of death. I have no sympathy for dying humans because they are insignificant grains of sand in a vast celestial beach.

Obviously angry, Rhea exploded. She said to Oscar, Don't listen to wicked Phobos's emphasis on emotion and fear. Certainly, if you hold back your emotions, you never experience them fully, so you naturally become afraid of death, pain, and grief and succumb to Phobos's trap. However, it is better to experience an emotion fully in order to know it and detach yourself from it. Doing so allows your intellect to intervene, superintend your emotions, and thus allow you to step away from emotionally driven fear. Put another way, fully feel the fear of death, and then let it go. This, by the way, is one key to accepting death.

Philosophy and Getting Old

Rhea then said, Compare philosophy's advice to those experiencing old age to Phobos's advice. Obviously, those closer to death are more aware of their mortality, so the eternal struggle to retain life and vitality and avoid decay and decrepitude becomes more acute. If you accept Phobos's fear-driven view, whatever remains of your life is ruined, along with the experience of death. You remain in paralyzing fear of death.

Philosophy and reason, as mentioned earlier, teach you to ignore the fear and use your intellect to keep your life interesting through challenges because you will then live a better and longer life and have an easier death. With this way of thinking, you resolve to stay well rather than resign yourself to die. You'll urge yourself to do what it takes to be well through exercise, drugs, and eating better food, to name a few things. One recent long-term study of humans offered a few interesting ways for them to live longer, some of which are obvious, like having good genes, not smoking, exercising every day, socializing, being romantically and sexually active, and remaining mentally active. Others are not so obvious, even counterintuitive, that only the intellect can discern, such as drinking alcohol in moderation, drinking coffee, gaining a little weight, and having moderately high blood pressure when old (because it prevents dementia). The study also demonstrated that food and vitamins made no difference to humans' longevity.

Philosophy also provides intellectual ways to accept the inevitable naturalness of death. It tells you that it will happen, so rather than rage against old age and death, embrace them. With these thoughts life becomes easier. You work less and play more, you relax and sleep better, and you enjoy more of what you can, like reading, relationships, dancing, and taking up a sport.

Rhea paused for a moment and then said, There is one intellectual among you humans who demonstrated this perfectly. She then summoned Chronos and asked him to bring William F. Buckley Jr. to them, which surprised Oscar because he had heard so much about him.

When Buckley arrived, in his trademark conservative grey suit, he was obviously amused. He said he had been following their conversation with interest and was honored to be asked to make a few comments. Buckley said that in his old age, he had feared losing interest in life because he knew it meant he was ready to die, a fearful thought at the time. He went on, However, in retrospect this was my initial emotional response to dying. But my intellect told me to fight to keep life interesting, which I did, and it gave me many more years of rich life.

Rhea pointed out to Oscar and resentful Phobos, Resisting aging is more poignant to thinking humans like Buckley than the unthinking ones who easily succumb to Phobos's emotional fears. She said, This is the difference between the emotional and intellectual response to dying. She then thanked Buckley for coming and Chronos for bringing him, and told Phobos to go away.

In conclusion, Rhea told Oscar, we have described some ways humans die and old age, so now let us describe what will kill you.

CHAPTER 14
Congestive Heart Disease

R HEA TOLD OSCAR SHE HAD ASKED ATHENA TO HELP HER describe the relation between instinct and death; Asclepius to describe Oscar's heart problems, including congestive heart disease, and dementia; Chronos to transport them to a hospital to talk with a congestive heart disease patient; and Apollo, who was prescient, to describe how Oscar would die when he got out of Limbo.

Oscar winced and said he was horrified to have someone describe to him in detail how he was going to die. He asked Rhea why she was torturing him by having Asclepius and Apollo describe his death.

The philosopher Rhea smiled at Oscar and said she was sorry if this disturbed him, but then asked why it was a problem because he, along with all mortal humans, knew that he would die. She said, It should not bother you, because your death is inevitable.

Oscar said, That is like telling someone who is about to be guillotined to relax because it is going to happen.

Instinct to Survive

Athena appeared at Rhea's request and said to Oscar, Instincts are biologically hardwired into humans for good reasons. She said, There are many instincts—including revenge, loyalty, greed, and empathy—but the four basic ones are fighting, fleeing, feeding, and sex. The last one, sex, is the urge to reproduce and replenish the species. The first three, however, are direct consequences of humans' most basic instinct, which is survival, or the powerful desire to live. The reason for the instinct to feed is obvious—without water you die within three days, and without food, twenty-one days. Fighting and fleeing, however, are instinctual reactions to danger. With these two instincts, when properly gauged, either way you win, by either fighting or fleeing.

The reason I describe these instincts, continued Athena, is because they are the radar that keeps you alive. Indeed, the survival instinct is the essential urge that preserves you. Without it, you would become languid and indifferent to life and danger, and quickly die.

One good example of this is the earlier description of your famous human William F. Buckley Jr. He knew he was losing interest in living, which collaterally diminished his survival instinct, and sure enough, shortly thereafter he died. I bring this up, Oscar, because it occurs to me that before you entered Limbo, you also were losing interest in living. For many reasons, but mainly due to your heart problems, you were finding it harder to live, which was diminishing your instinct to survive. Put another way, you were less interested in fighting or flying, which made you helpless, depressed, and ready for the grave. You were killing yourself long before Hades and Grimy got you to Limbo because you had given up, and death is the natural result.

Oscar had listened intently to Athena, who then told Oscar,

Asclepius will now discuss your heart issues, which are the cause of your slow spiral to the grave.

Congestive Heart Disease

Asclepius told Oscar, Apollo told me that you will die from congestive heart disease, or CHD, which is often called congestive heart failure, or CHF, when you get out of Limbo. The term *congestive* refers to the buildup of fluid in the ankles, feet, arms, lungs, and other organs. CHD is a killer of humans, taking about 6.2 million Americans each year.

Oscar was horrified to hear this. He told the gods, Living in Limbo is bad enough, but to have someone tell you exactly how you are going to die is painful. To make matters worse, Oscar continued, I am sure I have mild-stage CHD because I am experiencing some of the symptoms.

Asclepius said, Fine, Oscar, but I have more to say. Congestive heart disease is a chronic progressive condition that affects the pumping power of the heart muscle. Specifically, it refers to the stage in which fluid builds up within the heart and causes it to pump inefficiently. There are three stages of CHD: mild, moderate, and severe. The mild-stage symptoms are shortness of breath, heart palpitations with physical activity, and edema in the ankles and feet. *Edema* is a medical term that means swelling caused by excess fluid trapped in body tissues.

At the moderate stage, the heart begins to fail, weakness and fatigue are significant, shortness of breath and heart palpations occur with any physical activity, and the pulse is weaker due to the struggling heart. As a result, sufferers begin to limit their physical activity and rest more. At this stage the edemas of the hands and lower extremities, like the feet, become larger and more pronounced. Rings and shoes become tighter.

In severe or end-stage CHD, the symptoms become more severe as the sufferer progresses toward death. The heart and lungs have become so compromised that any physical activity makes the other symptoms worse, and fluid buildup in several areas of the body begins to back up into the lungs. Sufferers are increasingly exhausted and weak. At this stage CHD begins to affect the sufferer's mental state, which includes feelings of anxiousness, restless, confusion, and disorientation. They also experience a loss of appetite and find that the only way to sleep is to keep their head elevated on pillows in an upright chair.

Chronos then took Oscar, Apollo, and Asclepius to a local hospital to meet sixty-five-year-old Sean Ryan, who was dying from CHD. Sean was weak but glad to have company. He told them he had his first heart attack at age forty-five, had five stents in his coronary arteries, and he was in the hospital because of an irregular and rapid heartbeat. He told them, CHD is an awful disease to have. I have shortness of breath even without exerting myself. I must rest going upstairs, and just bending over to tie my shoes or pick things up off the floor makes me out of breath. I often wake up at night feeling like I cannot catch my breath. He showed them the massive edemas in his feet, ankles, and upper legs, as well as his swollen stomach. He complained of the weight he had gained—several pounds a week—and told them the only way he could sleep was upright in his La-Z-Boy chair.

Asclepius said thank you, and Oscar was silent. They learned later that Sean died suddenly shortly after their visit.

Back in Limbo, Asclepius told Oscar that he was particularly susceptible to getting CHD because of his heart attacks. He said, You had your first heart attack at twenty-eight, and they put in a stent. With your second attack at thirty-two, they did a triple bypass, and your third attack at thirty-eight was when you got a new heart valve. He told Oscar that with each of his heart attacks, a little of his scarred cardiac muscle died due to lack of blood. As a result, his heart was less able to pump blood, which made him a prime candidate to get CHD.

Symptoms of Congestive Heart Disease

Apollo, the prescient god of sun and healing, told Oscar he would describe the symptoms Oscar would have at the end of the severe stage of CHD and at his death from the disease.

Oscar told Apollo he would prefer he wouldn't, but Apollo continued.

At the end of the severe stage, your heart is failing. You will feel weak and fatigued, and you have chest pain, fainting spells, rapid and irregular heartbeats, and an enlarged, exhausted heart. Your breathing will become shallow and labored, and you will struggle to get enough oxygen even when resting. You will have a wheezing, chronic cough that will produce a white- or pink-colored mucus. Your edemas will become larger, not only in the legs and arms, but also in your abdomen, which will be bloated due to fluid collection inside your belly, like Sean Ryan's swollen stomach. Also, like Sean, you will gain three or more pounds a day due to your increased fluid retention. Your electrolyte levels will become abnormal, your urine will be dark as your kidneys begin to fail, and you will experience confusion, delirium, and disorientation due to your changing blood sodium levels.

Oscar was silent, and his face was pale white.

Dying from Congestive Heart Disease

Apollo and Asclepius then described to a dismayed Oscar what it would be like just before he died from CHD. Apollo told Oscar,

Your wounded, weakened, damaged, and failing heart can barely keep you alive. Your body is screaming for oxygenated blood, but your heart cannot pump hard enough to supply it. Your death will be slow and uncomfortable.

Your ability to breathe will become increasingly difficult as your lung tissue becomes more and more congested with fluid. As you approach death, your breathing will sound like rattling because your airways will become blocked. Your doctors will find it increasingly difficult to get rid of excess fluid in your lungs, belly, and around your heart, which only puts an extra load on your failing heart. With each breath, your death approaches.

Asclepius then said, The four common ways CHD can kill you are pneumonia, urinary infection, sepsis, and irregular heart rhythm.

Apollo told Oscar he would die from pneumonia.

Asclepius said, Your inflamed and waterlogged lungs will become a breeding ground for bacteria, and your lungs' air sacs will fill with fluid, which will starve you of oxygen. In the end, you will struggle to breathe and eventually succumb to asphyxiation. In effect, you will drown. Unfortunately, your dying from pneumonia will take longer than suddenly from a heart arrhythmia.

Oscar was frozen with fear. He said, What an awful way to die. The way you describe it makes it sound far worse than my heart attacks.

The Consequences of Knowing When You Will Die

Athena then told Oscar, It is telling to observe what humans would think if they knew the day, time, and place they will die, because it makes conspicuous how they ought to live in the present.

Oscar seemed puzzled. He said that earlier Apollo had told him how he was going to die, which was painful, but not where and when. He only said soon.

Athena said, Humans usually respond to this kind of knowledge in one of two ways, depending on the kind of character and world outlook they have. Angry-resisting humans, who mourn their death and feel sorry for themselves, and serene-accepting humans, who think about the good things in their lives, have been described. The angry-resisting types find such certainty unsettling, which makes them more fearful of death. It takes the spontaneity out of their lives, and they increasingly dread the passing of time as they get closer to the end. They are so self-absorbed they can only mourn their demise and feel sorry for themselves. These kinds of humans can only find happiness in ignorance—the ignorance of not knowing when they will die.

The serene-accepting humans have a very different reaction to knowing when they will die. Because they think of death as normal and thus accept it, knowing when they die does not matter. Their happiness does not come from the ignorance of knowing when they will die, because they had already accepted the fact that they will die. Knowing does not interfere with their natural, zestful, robust, and energetic life. When they are dying, these are the ones who have a party and use their money to buy their family gifts. If they had only two weeks left to live, they would wring the most out of their remaining time, quit their dead-end job, spend time with family and friends, do what they always wanted to do now, make a video of their lives for their descendants, and eat their favorite meals. If they had a year to live, they would think about leaving an impact, pursuing their life bucket list, and endeavoring to pass on some wisdom, if they have it to give, to future generations.

The point of all this, then, is to realize there never is enough time left to do what you want in life. You can never be satisfied. So the best solutions are carpe diem, or seize the day; do what you want now and not later; have joy, fun, play, gratitude, and adventure each day; and do now that which will create memories and bring smiles to peoples' faces.

Ways Humans Die

Asclepius then said, Earlier I pointed out that there are several doors for humans to exit life, so now let us describe one more door: dementia. *Dementia* is a general term for loss of memory, language, problem-solving, and other thinking abilities that are severe enough to interfere with daily life. The three most common types of dementia are Alzheimer's disease, vascular dementia, and Lewy body dementia. For now, continued Asclepius, I will describe dementia in general, and later Alzheimer's specifically.

Dementia is caused by damage to or loss of nerve cells and their connections in the brain. Dementia can occur quickly and suddenly get worse, or it can develop gradually over many months or years. It usually occurs in old people—about 14 percent of humans over seventy-one have some form of dementia.

There are seven stages of dementia: normal behavior, for-getfulness, mild decline, moderate decline, moderately severe decline, and finally very severe decline. The first signs of dementia are memory problems, especially remembering recent events, increased confusion, reduced concentration, personality or behavior changes, apathy and withdrawal or depression, and the loss of ability to do everyday tasks.

Oscar jumped to his feet and said he had known somebody who died of dementia.

Apollo was overheard whispering to Asclepius, I think Oscar is just glad we are not talking about him and how he is going to die.

Oscar said that dementia had drastically changed this person's character. He said he watched Roisin, an older woman in Palanga who he had befriended, lose her memory, and with it many emotions, like desire and hatred. He remembered seeing her with relatives and friends without enjoying them, and leaving them without regret. He said that as her dementia worsened, she did not rejoice in small pleasures. It was like life no longer interested her. Near the end of Roisin's life, Oscar said, because she had no memory, her life was erased. She grew indifferent to everything, nothing affected her, and she lost all hope. He said it was awful to watch her fade away like that.

Asclepius continued, At end- or late-stage dementia, the symptoms become so severe the patient requires help with everyday activities. This is a clear sign that they are near the end of their life.

In its later stages, those who suffer from dementia, Asclepius went on, usually exhibit numerous personality changes, such as wandering, hoarding, and other compulsive behaviors. However, the most troublesome behavioral changes are anger, aggression, and violence, which often put a spouse or caretaker at risk. This is due to the patient's loss of cognitive function, which frustrates them. They cannot articulate or identify the cause of their physical discomfort, so they express themselves through physical aggression.

Athena then said, Next let us talk about other aspects of human death. We will discuss death and desire, gratitude, old age, why humans should be satisfied with their own time, and why they should die in their own era, mostly from the perspective of the serene-accepting person described earlier.

A now-pensive Oscar said he was so fearful of dying that once he had considered suicide. However, even though the description of how he would die was dreadful, he was determined to accept it. He said he wanted to think like the serene-accepting type who reconciles with their death. But, he added, he would prefer the gods let him out of Limbo first.

CHAPTER 15
Old Age and Death

Oscar looked at the gods and said, Even though I am only forty-four years old, I feel older. He asked them if they would discuss old age, because he was suffering from congestive heart disease and believed he would die soon.

Chronos, the god of time, said, We have discussed humans' first thoughts on getting older and humans experiencing old age for the first time, so now let us discuss experiencing and struggling with old age and death. Later on, we will describe old age in general, desire and death, when ought we die, and counterintuitively, the gratitude humans should feel for having lived and died. A lot happens when you humans get old.

Metis then added, This topic has been of great interest to the ancient human philosophers, especially the Stoics, so we will be liberally quoting them.

Old Age
Wise Metis told Oscar that, depending on the era, old age does not really start until humans are sixty or seventy years old, but because

of his heart attacks, Oscar was exhibiting many old age traits at forty-four. She said, Old age is the end-of-life process, preparation for departure, decline, and ultimately mortality. It is a continuous series of losses where those who are aging never completely return to their previous state, which makes it a long, slow fade. When the loses surpass the repairs, it is the time for death has arrived.

Historically, she continued, surviving into old age was uncommon. In ancient Roman times, the average life expectancy was twenty-eight; in America in the early 1900s, it was under fifty, and in the 1930s, it was just over sixty. People did not live long, and those that did usually ended up in the poorhouse.

When It's Time to Go

Asclepius took over the conversation and said, Humans just fall apart in their old age. They become dry and brittle, their flesh sags, they shrink in size, their eyes bulge and sag, they find it harder to see due to cataracts, they lose teeth, they lose a quarter to half of their muscles, they lose their hearing and memory, and by age seventy their brain has shrunk so much there is almost an inch of spare room in their skull. Their posture changes dramatically when their neck and shoulders become stooped and contracted, and their lower spine gets an excessive inward curvature, called lordosis or swayback, that tips their heads forward. Their body loses its ability to maintain adequate blood pressure for their brain to function during changes in posture, like standing up from sitting. Sometimes they just pass out.

They suffer innumerable illnesses in old age. Emphysema, stomach pains, angina, heart fluttering, infections, urinary tract problems, hypertension, arthritis, and muscular dystrophy are just a few of the ailments that keep knocking on their spirit. Every year about 350,000 Americans fall and break a hip, 40 percent of whom end up in a nursing home and 25 percent of whom never walk again. They lose vitality due to reduced blood flow, and their bodies gradually atrophy. Overall, about 85 percent of old humans will succumb to one of seven diseases: atherosclerosis, hypertension, diabetes, obesity, mental depressing states such as Alzheimer's disease, cancer, and infection. These diseases prepare them for departure.

Problems with Modern Medicine

Koalemos, god of stupidity and ignorance, then spoke up and described how humans' modern medicine sometimes does the opposite of what it should do. Due to a variety of influences, he said—like the somewhat obsolete Hippocratic oath, technology, laws, hospitals, and insurance companies—modern medicine's goal is patients' living well, but it is often indifferent to their dying well. For example, hospitals routinely send patients who cannot do the eight essential activities (use the toilet, eat, dress, bathe, groom, get out of bed, get out of a chair, and walk) to a care facility. Indeed, about 50 percent of old people end up in end-of-the-line and often sterile nursing homes. On the contrary, doctors should help their patients have a good death. They should also honor their wishes, like the wish to die in their home.

Change in Attitude and Priorities

Metis said, Humans' attitudes and priorities change when they get old. They become more interested in people than things, in time than money, and in health than success. When they begin to actualize their death, their attitude usually makes them think either nothing matters because they will be dead soon, or everything matters because they don't have much time left. The former way may be realistic, but it goes nowhere. Indeed, Cicero wrote that *being tired of life makes the time ripe for death.*

The latter attitude is energizing because they focus on what really matters in life. A good way to demonstrate this change in priorities is Abraham Maslow's pyramid. Maslow was a famous human psychologist who, in his paper "A Theory of Human Motivation," described the levels of humans' growth and enlightenment over time. When young, humans focus on their basic needs, like food and water, which are at the bottom of the pyramid. As these are satisfied, they move up and become interested in love and belonging, and usually start reproducing. The next level is their desire for growth, and at the top is their striving for self-actualization, self-fulfillment, pursuit of moral ideals, and creativity for its own sake. It is not until they are old and don't have much time left that some of them reach the top of Maslow's pyramid. In a way, Maslow described what humans think makes life worthwhile.

It is ironic to observe, however, that when humans get very close to death, they often reverse course and descend the pyramid. They lose interest in self-fulfillment and creativity because they are either too tired or have already done it. They lose interest in growth because they are decaying. Their need for love and belonging remain strong, but most of their friends and some of their family are gone. Eventually they return to the lowest level, the need for food and water, because they are just glad they still can eat and drink.

Old age is the time to evaluate yourself, consider what is truly meaningful in life, and ask if you have been a moral person. In a funny way, if you had virtue, your death is more bearable than if you had not. Being without virtue often makes your last days an unbearable decline. I will discuss this later, with the view that death is in reality a liberating and pleasurable sensation.

Old Age and Death

It was then that Phobos, god of fear and panic, said, It's Grimy who keeps saying humans are fickle because they fear death. I've mentioned many of the reasons for this fear earlier, one being death's permeance. But, Phobos emphatically continued, humans should not fear it, which is a common theme among some of their famous philosophers. Cicero wrote, *To die is not an evil,* Epictetus *that the source of all human evils is not death but rather the fear of death,* and Marcus Aurelius that *departing from the world of men is nothing to fear.*

Metis then looked at Oscar and said, Earlier Elpis described a few reasons humans should accept death, so let me now give you more reasons, many of which have been mentioned by your philosophers.

Most Are Already Gone

First of all, Marcus Aurelius wrote that *many who have come are already gone.* Observe also that far more have already left this world than are living in it now. I am sorry to disappoint you, Oscar, but you just are not special, and after you die, you will soon be forgotten. Indeed, Epictetus wrote that *the world will not be turned upside down when one dies,* and Marcus Aurelius opined that *one will die and shortly after not even his name will be left.*

Nothing Can Happen to You When You Are Dead

Further, Metis said, Lucretius believed people should not fear death because when they no longer exist, nothing can happen to them. Earlier, the harm theory was described, which asserts that death is a harm if it harms your life in some way, such as preventing you from experiencing future joys. Certainly death may harm your future, but this is only if you are alive. If you are dead, it is irrelevant because nothing can harm you. Indeed, Marcus Aurelius asked, *Why you should fear being dead if it is a place where one feels no misery.* Lucretius wrote that *a person who does not exist cannot be miserable,* and contemporary philosopher Charles Hartshorne wrote that *in death, there are no more failures and disappointments.*

Put another way, why would you not embrace death? It, as Cicero wrote, *leaves us no further cares, anxieties for the future.* With death, you are relieved from troubles, or as Cicero put it, *When we depart from life…we are being set free from prison and loosed from our chains…to be free from sensation and trouble.* For Cicero, death is *a haven and place of refuge prepared for us.*

So, there you have it, Oscar. Dying should not be feared, because it frees you from pain and suffering. You just go to sleep and, unconscious and unconcerned, forget.

You Only Die Once

Metis then said, The next reason comes from one or your old human proverbs: remember that you only die once. Even if you fear death, at least you only have to do it once. There are many fearful human maladies that can recur, like depression, divorce, debt, and sickness, but thankfully death happens only once.

You Were Nothing Before You Were Born

Metis then asked Oscar, If you were nothing before you were born, why would you fear returning to that state when you die? She said, This is a popular common and profound theme among human philosophers. The ancient philosopher Seneca wrote that *in death it will be the same for one as before birth,* and that *death is all that was before us.* Lucretius asked, *If the vast amount of time before is nothing, why be distressed to return to it?* Recent philosopher Thomas Nagel asked, *When one accepts the fact that there was a time before they were born and did not exist, why should they be so disturbed at the prospect of a similar time after death?*

The truth is, Oscar, Metis continued, the world without you will just return to being without you again. It is the same, so it should not matter.

There are Worse Things than Dying and Being Dead There are worse things than dying and being dead. Being tortured, watching your young child die, and raising a teenager are worse.

To Be Nothing Is Good

Why is being nothing such a terrible thing? It is neither pleasant nor unpleasant because humans cannot experience it. Further, because humans have no control over whether it happens, why worry? The human philosopher Baruch Spinoza wrote that *a free man does not think of death; rather, [he] meditates on life.* So focus on life, make yours a good one, and accept becoming nothing.

You Were Born to Die

Your life's purpose is to survive and reproduce. To achieve this, most of your human lives are a hazardous advance through no man's land that inexorably ends in the valley of death. To live requires you to die. Just accept this reality and live fully while you can.

Why Fear Natural Death?

Earlier Phobos said that humans should not fear death, and one reason is because death is natural. Why fear something that is natural? Eating, sleeping, and sex are natural, and people do not fear them, so why fear death?

Many philosophers have described the cycle of life: birth–living–death. For them, it is a natural, timeless cycle that people should just acknowledge rather than fear. Epictetus wrote that *sensible*

corn would not want to be reaped, but sensible or not, corn natu-
rally dies, so why should sensible man curse natural death? He also
wrote that *bodies are not one's own; rather, they are nature's corpses.*
Marcus Aurelius wrote that *adults should accept death as a function*
of nature—only children fear nature's functions, and that *people are*
simply awaiting death as one of the functions of nature.

Eternal sleep is more real, common, natural, and attractive than
eternal life.

Old Age Is a Pleasurable Sensation and Death a Long, Calm Sleep

It was mentioned earlier that many humans find old age and death
a painful, unbearable decline. I find it ironic, asserted Metis, that
humans' philosophers argued that the opposite is true. Many
believed old age is a pleasurable sensation, a pleasant time of life
that all should enjoy, and death a long, calm sleep.

Cicero lauded old age because people can happily exit life. He
wrote that *ripeness, or old age, is so pleasant because the closer one*
comes to death the more he seems to come within sight of land, coming
at long last into harbor after a far voyage. For Cicero, *the end of life's*
voyage makes one ripe for death. Old age is like *the last act of a play*
in which, if one has had his fill of the play, he ought to make his exit.
He wrote that *death is sleep, [so] there is no loss and should thus be*
met calmly.

Seneca wrote that *people should not be disturbed by death because*
it is unnatural to hope for one more day. Indeed, if one thinks about
it, *death is like long, calming sleep after a very strenuous day.* He
mirrored many of his fellow Stoic philosophers' thoughts when he
wrote that *death is a kind of pleasurable sensation, a gentle fading out,*
and that people should cherish and enjoy old age because fruit tastes
most delicious when the season is ending. On death and nothingness,
he wrote, *At either end of life, there is deep tranquility.*

Later, philosopher Lucretius simply asked, *What is so bitter about sleep and repose?*

Living Is More Frightening than Death

The truth is there is uncertainty in living and none in death. If you must fear something, you have far more reason to fear living. Unlike being dead, being alive is dangerous and problematic. While alive, you could be drafted and killed in war, wrongly incarcerated, die an ugly death in a car accident, become deranged or destitute, and you could die from starvation or exposure. But in death, you can't be drafted, killed in war, wrongly incarcerated, die in a car accident, be deranged, be destitute, or die from starvation or exposure. Further, there is no pain to endure in death, you no longer need to care for your body, and you don't have to pay bills. In death, you are freed from that Sisyphean life of forever having to roll the stone back up the mountain.

Many human philosophers have echoed this theme. For Lucretius, thanks to death, *people become free from mental anguish and fear and find an end to their troubles.* Later, philosopher Thomas Nagel wrote that *death should be something to be afraid of only if one survives it.*

Metis said to Oscar, Ultimately these reasons not to fear death are irrelevant because you will die and there is nothing you can do about it. So when death is near, welcome it, and as Cicero so sprightly wrote, *When death looks [you] in the face, the only thing [you] can do is smile back.* So smile back at death.

Death and Desire

Dionysus thanked Metis for her explanations and self-consciously said, Everyone thinks I am a flake because I indulge in wine and pleasure. However, it is precisely because I indulge in those pastimes that I know a few things about desire and unhappiness.

Plato once wrote that desire causes unhappiness. Perpetually desiring what one does not have only brings dissatisfaction and a vague sense of empty yearning. What better way to eliminate such desirous yearnings than with death? As Cicero wrote, *Happiness comes when people have left their bodies behind and are free from all desires and envies—the burdens of care are relaxed.* Desire demands a reward and, as Lucretius wrote, *People think death is awful because it takes away the prizes of life, but it also takes away the desire for these prizes.* Indeed, as Seneca pointed out, *How nice it is to have outworn one's desires.* Death is the ultimate way to escape unhappiness due to desire, and as Marcus Aurelius wrote, *relief from...the flesh.*

Death efficiently solves the problem by removing the desire.

Be Satisfied with Allotted Time

With that, Dionysus and Metis retired to their Olympian couches. Mania, goddess of insanity and the dead, took over the conversation and said, Earlier Rhea asserted a good life does not depend on your length of days but rather on your use of time. A person may have lived long but lived little. So, she asked, how long should a human live? How long a life should a human be satisfied with? How long is their allotted time to live?

Mania said, It varies. Earlier Thanatos said humans have a natural life span of 100 to 110 years, but Metis told us earlier that in Roman times they only lived to age twenty-eight on average, and in the early twentieth century in America, they only lived to fifty or sixty on average. There are too many variables to say how long a human should live; indeed, some die young in an auto accident or war, and others live to be over a hundred, and medicine is constantly changing the equation. But how long should a lifespan be to satisfy humans?

Mania said, It is based on any things, like genes and environment, but also mental calculations humans make about their lives, which involves expectations. Based on actuarial tables, a young person living in America today could expect to live around 77 years, but a 70-year-old nonsmoking male expects to live to 83.5, an 80-year-old nonsmoking male expects to live to 87, and a 90-year-old nonsmoking man expects to live to 94 or 95.

However, except in unusual situations, such as a young man dying in war or young woman in childbirth, however long they live, humans should be satisfied with their allotted time. Let me explain why.

First, there are natural human generational periods, usually between fifty and one hundred years, and if you live beyond your period you are encroaching on the next generation's time. Lucretius explained it best when he wrote, *People must perish so future generations may grow, who in turn will follow.* Encroaching on the next generation's time only brings resentment from youth for denying them careers and resources.

Second, some wise human philosopher wrote, *What one has enjoyed is over, it is hateful to seek more, which itself would eventually perish.* Third, human philosophers have argued that people should be satisfied with their allotted time for a variety of reasons. Cicero wrote, *Die when nature says—those were the terms of the loan; Seneca do not fret about death before your eyes because it is unnatural to hope for one more day—every journey has its end, know that we ought to die,* and citing Virgil in the *Aeneid,* he wrote, *I have lived and completed now the course that Fortune long ago allotted me.* Epictetus pointed out that *the cycle of life ought not to be feared because people are restored again to the material whence they came.* Finally, Marcus Aurelius wrote that *one should be content with his allocation of time, and that we should pass through this tiny fragment of time in tune with nature and leave it gladly.*

Further, living forever would truly be horrible. You would find the strain, effort, stress, and anxiety of life unbearable for eternity. It would be like going to a play that never ends. Besides, you would get bored. Once you had experienced all the good things life has to offer, like movies, relationships, children, friends, meals, travel, conversation, love, work, books, sex, and music, you have experienced them. They lose their novelty over time. Imagine, for example, that you could live 1,000 years. You would be utterly bored because you would have experienced everything, nothing would be new, and you would just be doing the same old things over and over. Believe me, Mania continued, you would not like immortality.

The human philosophers have emphatically stressed that living forever would be hell. Seneca wrote that *a man is a fool who wishes to have lived a thousand years ago, and similarly the one who wishes he could live another thousand years...are the same—one did not exist and will not exist; neither period should concern him.* For Marcus Aurelius, *It would be just more of the same, and life would become wearisome and tiring; it makes no difference if one lives a thousand years because he will see the same things; and do not act as if [you are] going to live ten thousand years [because] death hangs over thee.*

With that, Metis told Oscar to remember Marcus Aurelius's wise advice: *One should leave gladly.*

Die in Your Own Era

Metis asked Oscar, if he had the opportunity to be frozen and later revived in the future, would he do it? Imagine, continued Metis, that you could be magically transported to a time two hundred years in the future.

Oscar thought briefly and then asked Metis, Why wouldn't I?

Metis smiled and said, You would not want to. It is better to die in your own time, your own era.

Metis then said, We have touched on this topic obliquely many times during this discussion. You have only so much time, if exceeded, you are encroaching on others time, and when your family and friends have passed, so should you.

Friedrich Nietzsche famously wrote that *everyone should die at the right time.* This means each person has an allotted time to live, a unique era of their own in which to be a child, develop friends, marry, have a family, become grandparents, and then die. It is a special time, and when it is over, they should die, which happens at the right time. If a person lives before or after their time, they are an outsider in others' time. Their parents, childhood friends, spouse, children, grandchildren, and even descendants would not be there.

It is true that the world is different outside your time, which makes you out of place. But the most important change is all of the relationships you had developed during your era would end, and when they are gone, you become a stranger. The original people in your life, the ones with whom you had experienced life first-hand, leave. Oscar, you for example are very close to becoming an outsider. Your parents, Jonas and Regina, died long ago, your son Mehal drowned, your youngest son Maurice died from amyotrophic lateral sclerosis, and I am sorry to tell you that your wife Madeline will die shortly.

Oscar went white, was silent for some time, and then asked, How soon will Madeline die?

Metis said, All I can tell you is soon.

After a time, Oscar said, When Madeline dies, I would not want to continue to live. I will be ready to go. He then said he remembered his parents, when they were in their seventies, talking about the dead people they had known—grandparents, parents, siblings, and friends. They would say that they knew more dead people than living ones, so it must be time to go. Oscar recalled that his parents died shortly after saying this.

Metis said, The point is for you to appreciate your unique time alive and accept death when it comes.

Gratitude

Athena thanked Metis for her discussion and said, Euphrosyne, goddess of cheer, joy, and mirth, will now discuss gratitude.

Euphrosyne looked at Oscar and said, I understands the natural gratitude humans have for life, but it sounds strange to say they should be grateful for death as well. Most humans are naturally grateful for life, but few if any are grateful for their death. She said, Mania will explain why they should be shortly, but for now I will discuss why they should be grateful for life.

Gratitude for Life

It is a rare and unique gift to be alive and conscious. Oscar, you should enjoy your life. John Adams asked, *Why be in haste, why do injury to the sweetness of living?* Ralph Waldo Emerson admonished humans to *view life more as a journey than a race.* Cicero wrote that one should *be grateful for the life he had and die with a song of rapture for the life he has lived,* and Epictetus that *people should say when they die that they are thankful for the time they got to use and are content with the time they had.* Enjoy the sweetness of life, and do not give it away to rushing.

It is also a rare and unique gift to be formed out of primordial muck, eventually through evolution, as a human and then to be perpetuated by ancestors. These ancestors of yours have followed the timeless cycle of birth-living-death that was mentioned earlier. It is a natural, wonderful, and quite interesting cycle that you, Oscar, have had the opportunity to experience and participate in.

This cycle also makes you an ancestor who will pass benefits on to future grateful generations.

How long humans live was discussed earlier along with the fact that, throughout human history, life was short. So many humans have died young from disease, famine, and war, never having the opportunity to grow old. You, however, live in an age of longevity. Even though you will die soon in middle age, Oscar, most humans would be grateful for the opportunity to live long as long as you. In many ways, old age is a blessing that few experience.

The gratitude you show for life when you die demonstrates your thankfulness for having lived. Indeed, Epictetus wrote that *we should say when we die that we are thankful for the time we got to use here and we are content with the time we had.* It was your wonderful Lucretius who wrote, *One should depart like a banqueter who is sated with life, and embrace untroubled quiet with calm of mind, having had a grand time and being grateful to be invited to the party.*

Gratitude for Death

Euphrosyne then told Oscar that Mania, the goddess of insanity and the dead, would discuss why humans should be grateful they die.

Then rude and possibly unbalanced Mania, with her twitches and stutter, told Oscar that she did not like humans, and it is she who was grateful they die. However, she said, Zeus told her to be nice, so she would try.

Mania began by telling Oscar that gratitude for death had been obliquely touched on earlier. It was mentioned that with death, humans no longer fear death, because they are dead, and they no longer have to worry about their futures because they have none. She then quoted some famous human, she condescendingly could not remember who, that wrote *We seldom see anybody who is not uneasy or afraid to live.* You humans are a strange lot, not only are you afraid to live but also afraid to die. Why? You should be grateful for both—especially that you die.

When you die you say goodbye to your life of drudgery. No more quarrels with others, no more fights with your spouse, no more divorce, no more raising rebellious teenagers, no more work and bosses, no more bills, no more debt, no more disapprobation from others, no more possibility of being fined or jailed, no more poverty, no more being robbed, no more being spurned—the list is endless. Jean-Paul Sartre once wrote that hell is other human beings, but with death other humans disappear, so no more unpleasant emotions like hate, anger, revenge, or jealousy. With death you also no longer need to worry about your health; indeed, you can't get sick because you are dead. I could describe more reasons to be grateful for death, but for now let me just say your death ends your life's struggles, disappointments, and tribulations. Epictetus wrote that *death enables one to escape life's troubles, which makes it every man's heaven and refuge.*

We have already discussed why you would not want to live forever, which death guarantees will not happen. But further, with death you no longer have to take care of your body. Your bodies must be fed, kept warm, allowed to eliminate, cleaned, medicated, provided with sleep, sexually satisfied, groomed, and exercised, to name a few needs. Death ends all that. Indeed, Cicero once wrote that *in death one escapes the shackles of the body and the chains of life.*

On an ontological level, with death there are no more horrific catastrophes or circumstances beyond your control to fear. War, pestilence, earthquakes, fire, typhoons, and carnivorous animals are of no concern. Also, wanting happiness is an enduring human desire that is often thwarted, but with death there is no need to be happy. With death there are no more cares or desires to frustrate you, there are no more life duties—like being loyal to a spouse, supporting children, and performing at a job—which eliminates your anxiety for the future. With death you are also freed from control by other humans, such as tyrants, and more recently the tyranny of the majority in your democracy. I think it was Seneca who said a tyrant is only master of my corpse.

You should think of death as a place of peace for the tormented and weary. Ivan Turgenev in *Fathers and Sons* wrote that *the noonday blaze dies away and is succeeded by the evening and then the night; and returning there, in peaceful retreat, the tormented and weary find their sweetest sleep.*

With that, Mania lightened up a bit. She came to sympathize with the woes humans endure, which made all the other gods roll their eyes. She looked at Oscar and said, Many humans think of death as an old friend who has come to extricate them from life's painful circumstances. Indeed, Cicero once wrote that *when people depart from life, they should joyfully and thankfully consider that they are being set free from prison.* Perhaps more poignantly, she concluded, that venerable Plato of yours wrote in his *Timaeus* that *his soul will be loosened from the bonds and able to fly away with joy when he dies.* You can learn from Plato, because he considered death a pleasure and not a pain.

Ways Humans Die

Mania then brought in the Algea, gods of pain and suffering, who told Oscar that Alzheimer's disease is a form of dementia named after Dr. Alois Alzheimer, who in 1906 observed abnormal clumps, or amyloid plaques, and tangled bundles of fibers, now call neurofibrillary, in the brain of a patient who had died from dementia.

These plaques and tangles are the main features of Alzheimer's disease.

Worried and trembling, Oscar said his wife Madeline was in the last stages of the disease, which Algea acknowledged with understanding.

Algea said, Alzheimer's is a brain disorder that slowly destroys memory and thinking skills as well as the ability to do simple tasks. It usually progresses through three phases, which could better be described as three degrees. The first mild phase involves impaired memory, wandering, and personality changes. The second moderate phase is characterized by loss of reasoning power, impaired language, and the inability to recognize family and friends. The third severe phase, when the afflicted is near death, involves memory loss, incomprehension, the inability to communicate, and finally the loss of instinctive and voluntary action. Physically, at this final stage, the brain has shrunk; the convolutions of the brain have atrophied and become shallow, compressed, and small; and the sufferer is bedridden and totally dependent on others.

Algea continued, They don't know exactly what causes Alzheimer's, but they suspect genetics, environment, and lifestyle are factors. It usually appears late in life, more than six million Americans over age sixty-four have it, and it is the seventh leading cause of death in the United States in older adults.

Despondent Oscar then looked at Algea and said he had watched this brain illness gradually take his beloved wife Madeline away. Reminiscing, Oscar said, Madeline and I had a favorite song, a kind of symbol of our love for each other. The song "It Is Time to Say Goodbye," means we say goodbye when one of us dies after many years of working as a team and raising children. It means our journey together in life has come to an end. Madeline started showing symptoms of the disease at an early age, around forty, and is now frail, bedridden, and without memory. The saddest thing about this disease for me is that Madeline actually said goodbye when she lost her memory. She has not known me for some time. Her body is here, but she is gone. It was hard for me to say goodbye.

It was saddening to watch this awful disease take my beloved, he continued. Early on I noticed her loss of memory, impaired movement, and worsening judgment, as well as some behavioral changes like sleeplessness, wandering, agitation, and anxiety. She began to complain about the loss of her sense of smell and poor vision. Madeline gradually lost all desires and aversions, showed no hatred or tenderness, was perfectly indifferent toward objects once dear to her, took no pleasure in seeing friends or family, and rejoiced in no pleasure. Nothing aroused her interest, the events of her life were of no account, and she had no remembrances and no hope. She is leaving me without regret because nothing affects her.

The doctors told me that the disease causes neurons to lose connections in the brain and die, which usually leads to death in seven to ten years. Near the end of the severe phase, they said Madeline's brain had shrunk and that she would most likely die from infection, like pneumonia, or a blood clot.

Alzheimer's is an insidious disease that steals memory and erases relationships because deep relationships depend on the ability to remember.

Oscar thanked Algea and said he had learned much from him on old age and death, to be satisfied with his time and era, and to have gratitude for both life and death. He also said he remembered Phobos saying humans fear death because it is permeant and eternal, but as good Stoics, they ought not. Oscar then said he had accepted his death, but that was for his own death, not Madeline's. Tearfully, he said, She will be gone forever, and I find it impossible to accept that. I do not want to live in a world without her.

Madeline died a few days later from pneumonia.

CHAPTER 16

Oscar's Death

OSCAR WAS DISTRAUGHT WHEN HE WAS SUMMONED TO MT. Olympus. He looked at the gods and said, My Madeline is gone. She died last night. Without hesitation he then told them he had always expected to go first, but now that she was gone, he wanted to die. He said that he once had dreaded death, but now both his mind and body wanted to pass. He said, My mind has transcended its fear of death and wants to slip easily, like the serene-accepting type, into the black sack. My body, after three heart attacks and now congestive heart disease, is just ready, with or without my mind.

Thanatos, Hygeia, Phobos, and Athena Discuss Oscar
Thanatos said he was greatly moved with Oscar's resolve and courage.

Hygeia said, I told you that Oscar would die young because he did not take care of himself physically or mentally.

Phobos added that Oscar was lucky to live as long as he did, considering his many heart attacks.

Athena then said, If Oscar truly has overcome his fear of death, and thus led a more meaningful life, I think we should release him from Limbo and send him to Heaven. He has suffered enough.

Thanatos said, Athena is right. He asked Oscar if he really had overcome his fear.

The Fear of Death

Oscar said yes. He said he no longer feared the mental and physical anguish, felt the intense fear and anxiety, or experienced the dread and profound sense of doom of a heart attack and death. He said he had come to accept—even look forward to—the emptiness and nothingness death embodies. He also said that he no longer used strategies to help him forget death.

Philosophically, Oscar said, he had come to think that it is the young and healthy who fear death because they are the furthest from it. The old and decrepit, like himself, usually welcomed it as an old friend. The closer you get to death, the more it seems like you are being welcomed home. He also said he now thought the world would be just fine without him.

Athena then reminded Oscar that she thought acceptance was critical to meaning, or that you don't fully live until you accept dying. She asked if he had intellectually transcended the silent controls from parents, school, and society, and whether he had become more serene-accepting and thus other-regarding.

Oscar smiled at Athena and said he thought so. He said he had come to think of death as normal and had accepted the notion that someday he would return to the elements from which he came. Oscar then said he missed his family and was looking forward to being with them, as well as his old friend Benas Savickis, who had long ago died of a heart attack.

With that, Thanatos asked Charon to find Grimy because it was time Oscar got out of Limbo.

Philosophy and Death Reprise

Athena said to the gods that she was impressed with Oscar's change in perception. She said, When we first met him, all he could talk about was his fear of the unknown and death. Now he is just ready, even eager, to go. She mused about this attitude of fate, death, and nothingness, and said that many human philosophers had commented on this inexorable connection. She said Cicero wrote that *death is an eternal refuge where nothing is felt*; Epictetus that *death is every man's heaven, it is his refuge* and *it makes no difference how we die because we must* and Seneca that *how much longer would you make life? The decision is fixed,* and *every journey has its end.*

Oscar Gets Out of Limbo

Just then a bedraggled looking Grimy, who had come from a strip club, said, Well Oscar, my old hard-to-kill-friend, I guess this time I take you. It looks like your time allotted by the Fates has expired, so I am here to guide your spirit to the next realm. The gods were amazed with your change in personality, so I am taking you to Heaven, where you will live in eternal joy with them.

Oscar said, Thank God, or gods! It is about time. He asked Grimy if he would see his family and friends.

Grimy said, Some of them. The rest—especially those religious ancestors of yours—are in Purgatory. However, we must wait a bit longer, because I cannot harvest you until you die.

How Old People Die

Asclepius then told the other gods that most old humans died from seven diseases, either singly or in combination: atherosclerosis, hypertension, diabetes, mental depressing states like Alzheimer's, cancer, and infection. He said arteriosclerosis and hypertension cause heart attacks and strokes, and together were the reasons for Oscar's heart attacks and now his congestive heart disease. Certainly there are other causes of death in old people, Asclepius said, like suicide, respiratory diseases, and obesity, but these seven are the main ones.

Oscar's Symptoms

Asclepius continued, Oscar's earlier congestive heart disease symptoms were mild. They included occasional chest pain, fainting spells, rapid and irregular heartbeats, a wheezing-chronic cough, and bloating. However, new symptoms have recently arisen that are harbingers of imminent death, which is why we called for Grimy. Oscar's breathing in particular has become labored and shallow, as if he cannot get enough oxygen. His extremities have become swollen, and there have been changes in his urination; in particular, his urine has become very dark.

Oscar's Death

As Oscar's symptoms revealed his body had entered the final stages of dying and preparation for departure. He was encouraged to go to a nursing facility because he was becoming feeble and needed help. Oscar vehemently said no. He did not want to die in some strange place with strangers. He said that he would die at home alone, with all the memories of Madeline and their children.

Oscar's Thoughts Just Before Dying

Like everyone who is dying, Oscar had a lot of final thoughts just before he died.

Hypnos, the god of sleep, who rarely talked, said, It is interesting to observe how similar these final thoughts are among sentient humans. Certainly, their last thoughts depend much on how they lived their lives. A bitter person, for example, may experience anger at those who embittered them. However, the most common thoughts of dying humans are the same in a young solider dying on the battlefield, an old woman in a nursing home dying from cancer, a condemned person waiting to be executed, and a person dying from an infection caused by Parkinson's disease.

Once they get over the consternation of becoming a corpse with no future, they begin thinking about the people they had known and loved during their lives. Oscar, for example, was thinking about his father, Jonas, and mother, Regina; his wife, Madeline, and children Megan, Mehal, and Maurice; his friends Benas; young Ugne, who had died from pesticide; and Aoife, the young Irish mother he knew, who died from cancer.

This often causes humans to wonder how their loved ones will fare when they are gone, which usually leads to the observation that their loved ones can care for themselves and that the world will be just fine without them. Similarly, they think about their responsibilities, like their jobs, but again realize someone else can shoulder them and that there is nothing wrong with shedding their responsibilities and slipping away.

They think about their life challenges and accomplishments. They ask themselves whether they had lived a good life, which sometimes leads to regret. They wish they had done something they always wanted to do but never did, they rue their failed relationships and not having a family. They often think they are tired of living—that nothing is new—and look forward to escaping. Many reproach themselves for their life's wrongdoings, but they usually forgive themselves and feel joy at being at peace with themselves.

Some imagine going to Heaven and others returning to nature. Many feel grateful they are leaving their problems behind, a sentiment that Cicero captured when he wrote, *When we depart from life, let us obey joyfully and thankfully and consider that we are being set free from prison and loosed from our chains...to be free from sensation and trouble.* They think about detaching from impermanent reality and are often anxious to get this last life duty done.

After listening to this, a calm and reflective Oscar told Hypnos that he had lived a good life, that he accepted his mortality and inevitable fate, and that he was at peace with the world. He said he had heard a dying singer named Nightbirde sing her poetic song "It's OK." Its sad message was that it is okay to be lost and die. He said the song moved him and that he was ready to go.

The Smells of a Dying Person

Grimy then took Oscar back to his long-unoccupied house after getting him out of Limbo. He told Oscar that he had to leave to harvest a few souls but would return within a couple of days.

When Grimy returned to Oscar's, his first reaction was to a repulsive collage of smells Oscar and his house were emanating. The house smelled old, musty, and stale, like the house of an old person. Oscar himself smelled like urine and infected bed sores.

Oscar had one very distinct smell, that of acetone, that Grimy knew well. He smelled like raw seafood, paint remover, or more distinctly, nail polish remover. This is what humans smell like just before they die. It occurs because a dying persons metabolism changes due to their deteriorating body, which is in the process of chemically breaking down. Healthy bodies use glucose for energy, which is broken down in a process called *glycolysis*. However, when a person is dying, there is a deficit of glucose, so their bodies burn fatty tissue in a process called *ketosis*, and acetone is one of the byproducts.

Grimy knew the smell well—the nail-polish-remover odor of death due to acidosis. He knew Oscar was about to die.

The Death of Oscar Uzgalis

Oscar was at home among photos of his departed family with Grimy, who was watching Oscar die, a scene he had seen many times. Oscar was emaciated, his ribs showed, and he was bedridden and very weak. The skin of his knees, feet, and hands was purplish, pale, grey, and blotchy, his neck and shoulders stooped, his eyes bulged, and he was swollen due to edemas. Oscar was in the severe stage of congestive heart disease: his heart was weak, fatigued, and failing.

Shortly, Oscar's flesh began to sag, his breathing became shallow and labored, he developed a wheezing-chronic cough that produced a pink-colored mucus, he lost more weight, his edemas became larger, and he became increasingly confused, even delirious. He developed an infectious fever due to pneumonia, and his urine turned dark due to his failing kidneys. Weakened, Oscar complained of stomach pains, angina, and rapid and irregular heartbeats. Grimy thought to himself that death would come quickly now.

It wasn't long before Oscar's breath became more labored as he struggled to move air in and out of his infected lungs. As he approached death, his breathing rattled because his airways were becoming blocked. With each breath his death approached. His damaged and failing heart could barely keep him alive. His body was screaming for oxygenated blood, but his heart could not pump hard enough to supply it.

Oscar was dying from pneumonia brought on by congestive heart disease. His inflamed and waterlogged lungs had become a breeding ground for bacteria. His lung's air sacs had filled with fluid, which starved him of oxygen. He was suffering asphyxiation—he was drowning.

Grimy then watched Oscar go through the process everyone experiences when they die. Oscar's heart failed, the circulation of blood stopped, his tissues began to die without oxygen, his brain began flickering out, and his vital centers gradually began to cease functioning.

Oscar then entered his agonal moment, his final breaths just before death. It began with a series of heaving gasps for air that slowly grew longer between respirations, until he stopped breathing altogether.

Now a corpse, Oscar's muscles relaxed, and his muscles' tone diminished so he quickly released stool from his rectum, urine from his bladder, and saliva from his mouth.

Oscar was forty-five years old when he passed into history.

Saddened, Grimy swung his scythe over Oscar and harvested him. Before returning to the strip club, Grimy escorted Oscar to Heaven. During their journey, Oscar described to Grimy his final thoughts.

Death as a Pleasurable Experience

Oscar excitedly told Grimy that he was surprised and thrilled to go to Heaven because he hadn't thought there was one. He said, Earlier Metis talked about the pleasant sensation of old age, but that is nothing compared to my pleasurable experiences of death. It was like being welcomed by an old friend. He told Grimy he had looked forward to the best parts of his dying experience, in which he felt calm and serene as he slowly slipped off into that long, deeply tranquil sleep.

Grimy thought to himself, Oscar sure doesn't fear death anymore.

Oscar said he experienced the same surreal slow motion as he had earlier, including the dimming lights, the black sack, his body separation, and the darkness that quickly became light. He also said he experienced the same kaleidoscope of images of dead people he had known. His grandparents, parents, wife, children, relatives and friends beckoned him to join them—only this time he did.

Oscar said he relished the familiar sense of peace and well-being. It was the same familiar, easy, comfortable, and pleasurable experience. He said the physical sensation of being coaxed into the tunnel felt transcendentally good, which brought mental ease and comfort. Oscar then exclaimed that his death felt wonderful, that he was finally at rest, and that he felt physically relaxed and at peace with the world. He said he was grateful that he was not yanked back into ugly reality, did not have to continue living, and that he had no more life problems to deal with.

Thanatos, who had been watching Oscar and Grimy, said, Like Oscar now, most people show no pain or stress at death and are only interested in forgetting and sleep. Indeed, one human described those dying as wandering, uncertain, unconscious, and unconcerned souls. Further, some naturally embrace death, like the unhealthy old, decrepit, pain-ridden, and bored, who die from natural causes. It is the healthy young who die from unnatural causes, like war and accidents, who fear death.

It looks, Thanatos continued, like Oscar has finally found his haven—his place of safety and refuge where he can gently fade out. He has, as Cicero pointed out long ago, finally arrived at his home port and final resting place after a long arduous voyage.

Oscar's Legacy

Thanatos then said, Recall how everyone reviled Oscar when he died the first time and Grimy took him to Limbo. Most of his family was glad to see him go; indeed, his only daughter, Megan, had nothing but scorn for her dead father. His wife, Madeline, was ambivalent; his brother Domantas said Oscar was not much of a brother; his brother's wife, Lina, was only interested in any inheritance; and all his friends, like Elijah Ballus, Benas Prudius, Connor and Cara Kelly, and Adomas Urbonas, either found his death an inconvenience, did not care, or were indifferent.

But it is different now. After his epiphany and effort to change his life and make it more meaningful, Oscar became a new, enlightened person who loved life and came to appreciate the people he knew. If they were here now, they would revere and miss him.

Oscar's Warm Corpse

Thanatos said, At the moment of death, all of Oscar's muscles relaxed, a state called primary flaccidity. His eyeballs flattened, his eyelids lost their tension, his pupils dilated, his jaw fell open, and his joints and limbs became flexible. Within minutes of Oscar's heart stopping, a process called *pallor mortis* began as blood drained from his smaller veins in the skin, which caused his body to grow pale. This process was more visible in Oscar due to his light Lithuanian complexion. Gradually his body became flat and toneless, and his corpse began to shrink to almost half its living size. With the loss of tension in his muscles, his corpse also began to lose elasticity and sag, which caused his joints, like his jaw and hips, to become pronounced. Oscar then began decomposing. With that, Thanatos reminded Grimy to send Oscar's corpse to the undertaker.

Grimy said goodbye to his old friend at the gate of Heaven, and the gods welcomed him to his new home and said our conversation on death has been most interesting.

CHAPTER 17
Oscar's Corpse and the Mortician

HADES, GOD OF THE DEAD AND KING OF THE UNDERWORLD, said, It looks like Oscar has gone to Heaven and his body has gone to the undertaker. I would have liked to have him come to the Underworld to be with me, but all I get is his corpse. Indeed, I think it was the human philosopher Epictetus who said, *your poor body is not your own—it is to nature a corpse.* Nature has reclaimed Oscar's body.

I know that humans revile corpses. They remind them of the ephemeral state of being alive. It reminds them that their living is the exception and being dead, or nothing, is the rule. Thus, corpses remind humans that they will die and be a corpse themselves some-day, which upsets them.

Also, when they look at a corpse, they think someone should be there to talk to them, but nobody is there and nobody talks back. They realize the person is gone, much like Oscar and his old friend Benas Savickis's corpse after he died in Oscar's arms. They realize they are looking at something meat-like, like a hamburger patty.

Compatibilism

Somewhat confused Hades then said, Earlier, Rhea argued that everything is materialistic and determined, which would mean there could be no nonmaterial soul of Oscar that could go to Heaven.

Rhea responded, It turns out that the free will and determinism debate was a false dichotomy. They really are compatible. Humans have no control over some things, like whether they die, but some control over other things, like when to go to bed. This new compatibilism allows for Descartes's dualism—a body and a soul—so it may be possible for Oscar's soul to go to Heaven.

Elated Elpis, the god of hope, who had argued for a soul, shrieked with joy. When he heard the news, Baron d'Holbach, the strict determinist, was mortified.

Oscar's Corpse: Early Stage

The Walk of Honor

Here is Oscar's corpse, or what is left of it. He had donated his organs to others, so after the surgeons were done with him, his corpse was without many organs. He selflessly gave them to others so they could live. They had offered Oscar the walk of honor, where donors are solemnly wheeled down a corridor lined with medical people, relatives, and friends who honor them and say goodbye. Oscar declined the offer because he thought it was unnecessary.

The Smells of Oscar's Corpse

Earlier, Grimy had described how dying humans smelled like nail polish remover, but that is nothing compared to how they smell after they die. There is a reason humans quickly embalm or bury their dead: the smell of a decomposing dead body is intolerably noisome because they emit extremely offensive sulfury, rancid, and putrid smells, just like decaying meat. The noxious smells are like rodent urine, decayed steaks, a dumpster six months after a barbecue, and a dog's fart after he's gotten into the diaper pail.

Within an hour Oscar's corpse started emitting a potpourri of awful smells. The compound putrescine produced a cadaverine smell like rotting flesh, and his decomposing body began smelling like rotting meat with fruity undertones. A white or brownish crystalline solid produced by his corpse called *skatole* emitted a strong fecal odor. A crystalline chemical found in his intestines and feces called *indole* produced a mustier, mothball-like smell. Like all humans, when Oscar died, he lost bowel function due to muscle relaxation, so he peed and pooped, which emitted the smell of urine, and the hydrogen sulfide in his feces smelled like rotten eggs. His corpse also produced a colorless gas called *methanethiol* that had a distinctive putrid, rotting cabbage smell. It also produced dimethyl disulfide and trisulfide, which have a foul, garlic-like odor similar to sun-heated poop. On top of all this, at his death, like most humans, Oscar vomited the contents of his stomach, which brought the smell of gastric gases—a kind of nauseating, sweet smell. I should mention that hospice centers, nursing homes, and hospitals are inundated with these smells.

I should also mention the variety of colors Oscar's corpse goes through. First it was pink before death, then yellowish, then bluish-purple, then green, and then red before finally turning black. I will explain why shortly.

Why Human Corpses Are Eerie

Hades said that he always found humans' revulsion at a corpse curious. He said, Corpses are only natural, but humans make more of them than any other species. There are a number of reasons for this, one of which is the thought that they will look and smell like the corpse someday, and another is that the person who was the corpse is gone forever. This becomes particularly eerie when there has been a long relationship with the deceased person. It is hard for a husband, for example, to fathom looking into the unexpressive face of his dead loving wife of fifty years—a face that no longer responds to him.

A corpse also reminds humans of the finality of death. The person who just existed is gone forever. They also think that a corpse is an entity that has no cares, no future, and no plans, unlike them. Some find the corpse gross because it smells of pee and poop, and looks disgusting. They also realize the corpse is going to decompose and be returned to the elements, and that in the ground it will become food for maggots and worms, which will happen to them, which they find repellent.

Oscar's Corpse: Middle Stage

Before describing the progression of Oscar's dead body let me first broadly describe the decomposition process.

Oscar's Decomposition: Autolysis

Oscar's body began decomposition about four minutes after he died, and it will progress through four stages: autolysis, bloat, active decay, and skeletonization.

Autolysis is the first stage of decomposition, or self-digestion. As soon as Oscar's blood circulation and respiration stopped, his body had no way of getting oxygen or removing wastes. So excess carbon dioxide was produced, creating an acidic environment and causing membranes in cells to rupture. These membranes released enzymes that began eating the cells from the inside out. Small blisters filled with nutrient-rich fluid begin appearing on his internal organs and his skin's surface. His body thus developed a sheen due to ruptured blisters, and his skin's top layer began to loosen.

The First Twelve Hours after Death

At the moment of death, many physical changes started taking place in Oscar's body. It began to shrink, and his skin began losing it elasticity. During the first hour, his body cooled from its average temperature of 98.6 degrees Fahrenheit by about 1.5 degrees per hour until it reached the ambient temperature around it in a process called *algor mortis* or *death chill*, which is *cold death* in Latin. Forensic scientists use this process to determine the approximate time of death.

Because Oscar's eyes were his window to the world, what happened to them after he died hauntingly describes his now-closed window. At death the pressure in his eyes started to decrease. They became flaccid and began to sink into the orbits of his eyes. It takes muscles to open and close eyes, so because his muscles no longer worked, his eyelids popped open instead of staying closed (which is probably the reason for the ancient custom of placing coins on the deceased's eyelids: to keep them shut). His pupils became frozen, his eyes turned blue or grayish due to corneal opacity, and a hazy film formed over his eyeballs. They also began to flatten, turn milky, and roll up and back, exhibiting only the whites of his eyes. After two hours his cornea lost its reflex and became cloudy.

At two hours after death, because Oscar's heart no longer pumped blood, gravity began to pool blood to the areas of his body closest to the ground in a process called *livor mortis*. Oscar's body remained undisturbed for several hours, so those areas also began to develop a reddish-purple discoloration that resembled a bruise due to the accumulating blood. Embalmers sometimes refer to this as the *postmortem stain.*

At three hours after death, rigor mortis, or the stiffening of Oscar's body (especially his muscles), began. The first muscles affected were his eyelids, jaw, and neck.

At five hours after death, rigor mortis spread to Oscar's face and down through his chest, abdomen, arms, and legs, until it finally reached his fingers and toes.

Oscar's corpse reached maximum muscle stiffness at roughly twelve hours after death. His limbs were difficult to move, his knees and elbows were slightly flexed, and his fingers and toes appeared unusually crooked.

Oscar's Corpse: Late Stage

At thirteen hours after death, after reaching the maximum state of rigor mortis, Oscar's muscles began to loosen due to continued chemical changes within his cells and internal tissue decay. His corpse then began a process known as *secondary flaccidity*, which occurs over a period of one to three days. His body became more flaccid, like it had been at the time of his death, and his muscles again began to relax. Also during secondary flaccidity, his skin began to shrink, creating the strange illusion that his hair and nails were growing. Rigor mortis then dissipated from his fingers and toes as well as his face over a period of forty-eight hours.

One to Five Days after Death

Twenty-four hours after death, Oscar's internal organs began to decompose, and his skin turned a greenish color. At three to five days after death, his body started to bloat and blood-containing foam began to leak from his mouth and nose.

Oscar's Decomposition: Bloat

At three to five days after death, the second stage of Oscar's decomposition began: bloating. Leaked enzymes from the first decomposition stage began producing many gases, sulfur-containing compounds released from bacteria caused his skin to discolor, and his corpse doubled in size due to gas. Most corpses at this stage have insect activity, but Oscar did not because he was in a morgue.

The microorganisms and bacteria that had invaded Oscar's corpse started producing an extremely unpleasant odor called *putrefaction*. He began to really stink.

Eight to Ten Days after Death

Eight to ten days after death, Oscar's corpse turned from green to red as his blood decomposed and the organs in his abdomen accumulated gas.

Oscar's Decomposition: Active Decay

At ten to twenty-five days after death, Oscar's corpse entered the third stage of decay, active decay, which was evidenced when fluids began oozing from his orifices. His organs, muscles, and skin started liquefying, and his corpse's soft tissues began to decompose. His hard tissues, like hair, bones, cartilage, and other byproducts of decay, remained. During this stage his corpse lost the most mass.

Thirty Days after Death

Several weeks after his death, Oscar's nails and teeth began to fall out and his body continued to liquefy.

Oscar's Decomposition: Skeletonization

The fourth and final stage of Oscar's decomposition, which started around fifty days after his death, is skeletonization. This is the final stage, during which the last vestiges of the soft tissues of his corpse decayed or dried to the point where his skeleton was exposed.

So, after a couple of months, Oscar's body was largely decomposed and returned to the elements from which it came.

The Mortician

Grimy took Oscar's corpse to Albert Caldwell, a mortician. Albert asked Grimy what he wanted him to do with it. He said, There are three common ways of handling corpses. The first is do nothing and bury it as quickly as possible, which is common in war. The second is to embalm it if the funeral is to be open casket. The third is to cremate it so it can be put in an urn to be placed on someone's mantel.

Grimy explained to Albert that the gods wanted to embalm Oscar's corpse for his open-casket funeral.

Embalming Oscar's Corpse

Albert said, The first thing we will do is take off Oscar's clothes and place his corpse on a table, where it will be bathed, disinfected, and cleaned. We then cut his veins and drain about 1.5 gallons of his blood into a sink that goes into the sewer system and sewage treatment plant.

Grimy, who had seen much death in his time, shuddered. Even he thought it strange to unceremoniously dump Oscar's life-sustaining blood like old oil.

Albert then said, Next we seal his anus—and the vagina, if it is a woman—with cotton to prevent embalming fluid from leaking out. We then use an embalming machine, which looks like a blender, to inject a combination of water and preservative chemical, such as formaldehyde, into Oscar's corpse. This preservative fluid slows Oscar's corpse's decomposition.

There are two phases of embalming, arterial and cavity. Arterial is when the blood is replaced by embalming fluid, and cavity is when the fluids of the organs are replaced with embalming fluid. This prevents decay and fluids leaking from the body before burial or cremation. In cavity embalming the embalmer uses a device called a *trocar*, or hollow tube with a point on one end and a seal on the other, to puncture Oscar's stomach, bladder, large intestine, lungs, and other hollow organs, and suction is used to aspirate out the fluid and gas that has accumulated. The embalmer then pumps embalming fluid into Oscar's torso, and the puncture holes are sealed with a small plastic cap called a *trocar button*.

Because rigor mortis has set in, Oscar's limbs are massaged and his joints worked so they are movable. Next, we set Oscar's facial features. Facial stubble is shaved, and his eyes are closed using glue or small plastic eye caps that sit under the eyelid. Then his jaw is wired or sewn shut so his mouth can be arranged into a desired expression. After this process Oscar's corpse becomes a cadaver.

Cremating Oscar's Corpse

Albert told Grimy, Cremation is just the methodical and thorough burning of Oscar's corpse. First, we remove some mechanical parts, like pacemakers, beforehand because they may explode in the intense heat. We then put Oscar's corpse into a cremation chamber, called a *retort*, which is fueled by natural gas, oil, or propane, and heat it to a temperature of between 1,400 and 1,800 degrees Fahrenheit. It will take about one to three hours for Oscar's corpse to be reduced to about three to seven pounds. This makes his corpse into dried bone fragments and basic elements, and the gases made during the process are discharged through an exhaust system.

The cremator then crushes Oscar's remains with a long hoe-like rod and collects them in a tray and where they're allowed to cool. We remove and dispose of all non-consumed metal objects, like screws, dental work, prosthesis, implants, and jewelry. After that his dried bones are further ground into a finer sand-like consistency in a machine called a *cremulator*. The cremated remains are usually pasty white in color. Finally, Oscar's remains are put in an urn or plastic box.

Oscar's Grave

Albert then told Grimy, Because Oscar has no immediate living relatives, they will send his processed cadaver to the Lithuanian family cemetery, Palanga Cemetery in Lithuania, where all Uzgalises have been buried.

The cemetery overseers held an open-casket funeral for anyone who wanted to say goodbye to Oscar, one of whom was Grimy. Oscar was then interred in a prearranged plot next to Madeline and their children Megan, Mahal, and Maurice. He was also near his parents, Jonas and Regina Uzgalis, and many ancestors. Oscar was now at his eternal resting place.

Grimy then said goodbye to Oscar and left to gather another human.

CONCLUSION
The Gods' Final Thoughts

AS IN THE BEGINNING, THE MYTHOLOGICAL GODS AND GODDESSES were lying on their favorite lounge chairs high on Mt. Olympus discussing humans. They were still wondering why humans fear death, but this time they were ruminating on what had been said about the topic, which has been faithfully recorded in this book. There were many of them, but the main interlocuters were Zeus, god of lightning, thunder, and the heavens and leader of the Olympic gods; Thanatos, god of death; Athena, goddess of wisdom; and Phobos, god of fear. Grimy, the Grim Reaper and mythological harvester of humans, was an observer.

Phobos said, the topic has been humans' greatest fear, which is the fear of death, but it has also been about what it means to live.

Athena commented that exploring these topics was made real because they had followed the life and death of a real human, Oscar Uzgalis, who experienced them.

Asclepius said it was also made real because the numerous ways humans die had been explained, whether they be god, nature, humans, or animals. In Oscar's case it was death by heart disease. Oscar, continued Asclepius, was a good example to use because he initially feared death, a fear that had deceived him, put him in solitary confinement, and prevented him from living a meaningful life.

Athena nodded in agreement and added, Oscar had to overcome his fear of death in order to live a meaningful and fuller life.

Panacea commented that it was the discussion on meaningfulness, or what constitutes the good life, that was enlightening. It included the need to discover that meaning comes from within and not from some exterior source. She continued, Success judged by society comes at a great moral cost, and if Oscar had decided to pay that cost, his life would have remained hollow and insincere. But he did overcome his fear in the end because he realized death is natural and that all the strategies humans use to avoid it fail. He also realized that he would not want to live forever, that most of those he knew were already gone, that he only dies once, and that he was not fearful of being nothing because he already had been nothing before he was born.

Ares, the god of courage, then spoke up and said, It takes courage to overcome the fear of death.

Immediately Rhea, Athena, and Metis said in unison, Certainly, and it is philosophy and wisdom that teach courage.

With that Koalemos, the god of stupidity and ignorance, who was obviously agitated, said, The best way to avoid the fear of death is through ignorance. He quoted poet Thomas Grey, who wrote, *Ignorance is bliss,* and said, the best way to avoid something unpleasant is to not learn about it. Phobos agreed.

This ignited Rhea's ire. She said, Ignorance and emotionally driven fear are not the way to overcome fear. Recall how the famous human intellectual William F. Buckley used intellect to overcome fear. In his old age, he feared losing interest in life because he knew it meant he was ready to die, but his intellect told him to fight to keep life interesting, which he did, and it gave him many more years of a rich life. She said, Thinking humans who use reason, philosophy, and wisdom, like Buckley, are far more able to overcome the fear of death than Koalemos's and Phobos's emotionally driven detached ignorance.

Zeus then said, It is time to bring this discussion to an end.

Euphrosyne, the goddess of good cheer, joy and mirth, said, Let me tell you that Oscar greeted death as a welcome old friend.

Rhea said that she was glad to hear that but she knew, even after all this discussion, that humans cannot know death. Indeed, she said, it was Tolstoy who had raised the question about fear and death, and who poignantly wrote that you cannot understand the meaning of life so just live, the only thing that is true is death, everything else is false.

Zeus said, Good point, and left.

As the gods were leaving, I, the author of this book, got a chilling look from Grimy, who said, Your time has come to be gathered. I pleaded with him to let me finish this book. He said, You have

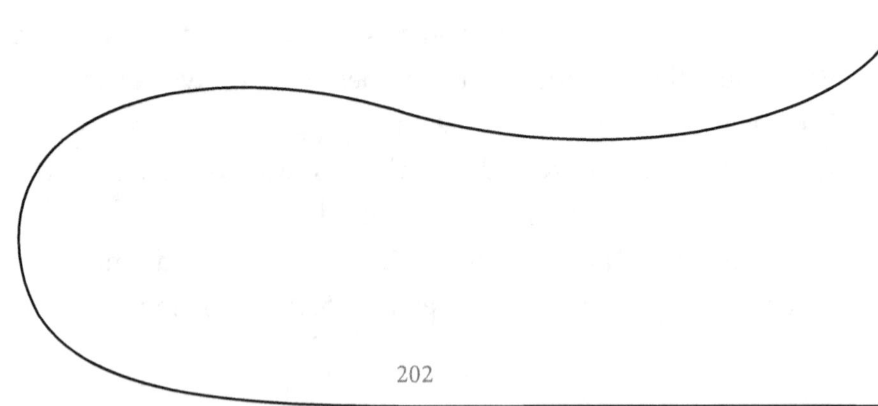

GREEK GODS AND GODDESSES

F OLLOWING ARE THE OLYMPIC GODS AND GODDESSES USED IN this book along with their titles. For interest, I have added some of their pronunciations in parentheses. The phonetics of their pronunciation may not be scholarly correct; rather, it is how I pronounce it.

Aether: god of light and the atmosphere (ee-thur)

Algea: gods of pain and suffering (al-jay-ah)

Apollo: god of the sun and healing

Ares: god of courage, chaos, and war (air-ees)

Asclepius: god of health and medicine (escape-ee-iss)

Athena: goddess of wisdom

Chaos: god of nothingness (kay-os)

Charon: the ferryman of Hades across the river Styx (care-on)

Chronos: god of time (karen)

Dionysus: god of wine and pleasure

Elpis: the spirit of hope (l-piss)

Aphrodite: goddess of love and beauty

Euphrosyne: the goddess of good cheer, joy and mirth (you-fross-a-knee)

Gaia: goddess of the earth

Grim Reaper: mythological harvester of humans

Hades: god of the dead, king of the Underworld

Hera: goddess of women, marriage, family, childbirth, and hearth (hair-a)

Hygeia: goddess of cleanliness and hygiene (hi-gee-aa)

Hypnos: god of sleep (hip-no-se)

Iaso: goddess of remedy (ee-a-so)

Koalemos: the god of stupidity and ignorance

Kratos: god of strength and power (cray-tose)

Mania: goddess of insanity and the dead (main-e-uh)

Metis: goddess of wisdom (meth-ese)

Mnemosyne: goddess of memory (men-oz-a-me)

Momus: god of satire, writers and poets (mo-mus)

Nemesis: goddess of retribution, vengeance

Nyx: goddess of the night (nukes)

Panacea: goddess of universal remedy

Phobos: god of fear and panic (fo-bos)

Plutus: god of wealth (plu-tus)

Poseidon (also Neptune): god of the sea and earthquakes

Priapus: god of gardens and fertility (pri-a-pus)

Rhea: goddess of nature (ray-a)

Thanatos: god of death (tan-a-toss)

Tyche: goddess of fortune and prosperity (tie-key)

Zeus: god of lightning, thunder, and the heavens, leader of the Olympic gods

ACKNOWLEDGMENTS

I USED MANY SOURCES TO WRITE THIS BOOK ON DEATH. IN CHAPTER eight, I used thanatologist David Moller's website, in particular the comments of Aoife, a fictional person repeating a real person's words who was dying from cancer. I embellished a few of the comments. In chapter eight I also used the *Encyclopedia of Death and Dying*.

In chapter ten I used Daniel Dennett's *Consciousness Explained* for Grey Walter's precognitive carousel.

In chapter twelve I used wording from *Tuesdays with Morrie* in "Attitude Toward Death."

I used Sherwin B. Nuland's *How We Die* throughout the book but mostly in chapter thirteen. The description of being mauled by a lion in chapter thirteen was taken from *The Guardian* on the internet. For chapter thirteen I also used Matthew Walker's *Why We Sleep*; on Michael Corke, I used *Neuroscientifically Challenged, Know Your Brain: Fatal Insomnia*, from Google, and a *60 Minutes* piece for philosophy and getting old.

In chapter fourteen I again quote liberally from Sherwin B. Nuland's *How We Die*. For chapter fourteen I used information from psychologist Jeff Harry's website on what we would do if we knew when we were going to die, and for information on congestive heart disease and dying patients' testimonials from the internet, I used eMedicine's "Congestive Heart Failure."

I again used Atul Gawande's book *Being Mortal: Medicine and What Matters in the End* in chapter fifteen.

Some general sources for the book include Ernest Becker's *The Denial of Death* and Thomas Nagel's excellent philosophic book *What Does It All Mean*. I quote philosophers, and particularly Stoic philosophers, in chapter fifteen and throughout the book. Most of the ideas and quotes come from my books *Philosophy and Happiness* and *A Reference Guide to Stoicism*.

I used Google extensively for the book. In chapter eleven I used actual comments from Google on soldiers writing home on death, which I sometimes paraphrased and/or embellished. I also used Google for near-death experiences, Phineas Gage, the anaconda snake constriction, and the previously mentioned woman's description of being mauled by a lion.

On vocabulary in chapter seventeen, I should mention a corpse is a dead human body, a cadaver is the medical term for a dead body human body that has been processed, and a carcass is the dead body of an animal.

I would like to thank Kristen Hall-Geisler, for editing, and Jenny Kimura, for interior and formatting, of Indigo: Editing, Design, and More. I would also like to thank my wife, Kathy Bowman, who gave me many ideas for the book, especially after a couple of martinis.